Wyatt Steele

The Silent Gunfighter

First published in eBook
and paperback 2024

PREFACE

Wyatt Steele's great grand pappy came from Dublin. A writer by trade, Declan Kelly had worked on the Irish Times and the so-called Freeman's Journal, reporting on politics and social injustice. In the late 1880's he crossed the Atlantic, arriving in New York he secured work with the Herald Newspaper. The newspaper regularly carried sensational stories, and so Declan headed out West to find some new material for the Herald.

During his travels Declan met many people, and he recorded their lives in his diaries. These are not tales of the old West; these are the firsthand reports from those involved of what happened. Most of the details in the diaries never made it into print. The diaries were passed to my father's father, then to my father and then about ten years ago to me. I'd heard some of the tales they included recounted to me by my father and grandfather in years gone past, but reading them again, and finding new stories of the lives of those long since gone, of the hardship they endured made me want to share these with those interested in this time period. This is the first, and hopefully not the last, of the stories from my grand pappy's diaries. The people you will read about in the following pages existed, the struggles they endured very real, this is not a work of fiction but a recount of an incident in their lives that shaped them.

This book is written in the style of the classic western, but remember, as you turn the pages that the events happened, they are based on the recollections of those who survived. The hopes, dreams, pain and fear were once felt by these people in a very real sense. Their experiences were written down when the events were fresh in their minds and their nerves still raw from what had just happened. Declan frustratingly only ever referred to those he wrote about by their initials. In this tale we have N & LC. These have become for this fictional re-write – Nash and Matt Cain.

Wyatt Steele

Contents

The Silent Gunfighter

Wyatt Steele

Dedicate to Luke Cain

INTRODUCTION

The cowboy's heart hammered as he urged his mare forward, her hooves pounding the hard, dusty earth with each desperate stride. Behind him, the yelping and chanting of the Comanche grew louder, carried on the hot wind that swept across the plains. His mare's breath came in labored gasps, her coat slicked with sweat that darkened her dun flanks. He could feel the strain in her muscles, the stumble that warned him she was reaching her limit.

"Come on, girl," he whispered, gripping the reins tightly, hoping his voice might lend her the strength she needed. But he knew better. Their mounts were fresher, tougher. The Comanche had planned this chase well.

A rocky ridge loomed up ahead—a steep, jagged wall that climbed into the open sky. It was his only chance, the only terrain rough enough to give him any advantage. With a firm press of his boot, he guided the mare toward the escarpment, feeling her legs falter beneath him. She stumbled once, caught herself, but her steps were growing sluggish, each one heavier than the last.

Another war cry split the air, closer this time, the sound slicing through his heart with the grim certainty that they were almost upon him. His mare struggled up the slope, her legs slipping against loose rock as she clawed her way forward, spurred on by instinct alone. But as they reached the edge of the escarpment, she gave a final heaving breath, stumbling to a halt. She could go no farther.

He dismounted, his own legs trembling as he steadied her with a hand to her neck, feeling her heaving breath beneath his palm. "You did good, girl," he murmured, and then, taking one last look at the oncoming riders, he turned and ran.

The rocky outcrop offered a scattered maze of boulders, the kind of cover he could work with if he could only reach it. The cowboy darted between the first few rocks, feeling his pulse hammering in his chest, each step echoing through the ground as he pushed his body to its limits. But the sound of hoofbeats bore down on him, growing louder with each stride he took.

A shout, a laugh—he felt the presence of one of them closing in, almost beside him now, a flicker of movement from the corner of his eye. He barely managed to twist around in time to see the warrior lunging toward him, a sinewy arm reaching out, and then he was thrown off his feet, tumbling across the hard ground. Pain shot through his side as he hit the earth, his vision blurring for a moment as he lay there, gasping for breath.

The Comanche were on him before he could move, their laughter and taunts filling the air as they surrounded him. He tried to sit up, but a moccasin clad foot struck his chest, pinning him down. One by one, they ripped away his guns, his knife, every last bit of steel he'd fought to keep close. Someone grabbed him by the collar, hauling him up to his knees, and he felt fists connect with his jaw, his ribs, each blow landing with a dull, bone-jarring ache.

Their words were a rough, guttural language he didn't understand, but their meaning was clear enough. They were enjoying this—relishing his helplessness, his pain. One of them slapped him hard across the face, the world tilting as he staggered back, only to feel a hand grip his collar again, wrenching him upright. They mocked him, the cruel smiles on their faces bright even in his blurred vision.

Finally, dazed and bloody, he was dragged to his feet, his wrists bound tightly with rough rawhide. He tried to resist, to twist free, but a solid fist caught him in the gut, knocking the wind out of him. He doubled over, his legs buckling beneath him as they hoisted him up, tying him tightly, the rawhide biting into his skin.

Then, with a sneer, they slung him across the saddle of his exhausted mare, his head hanging over her side, every bump of her ribs sending fresh waves of pain through his battered body.

They were mounting up, preparing to leave, when one of the Comanche made a sound—a low warning, sharp and urgent. The group froze, their laughter fading as they turned to follow his gaze, looking out across the horizon.

There, silhouetted against the setting sun, a lone figure sat astride a horse, watching them from a distance, a rifle cradled in his arms.

CHAPTER ONE

The prairie stretched out endlessly before him, a wild, unbroken land that seemed to go on forever under a vast, open sky. Nash rode with a quiet purpose, his shoulders hunched slightly as if he carried the weight of every mile on his back. There was a certain relief in solitude, he thought, a comfort in the wild plains, where no one looked too close, and no one cared to ask questions.

He was a man divided, his blood both white and Apache, yet accepted by neither. He'd seen firsthand how quickly townsfolk could turn on someone who didn't fit neatly into their world, someone who looked just a shade too dark, whose quiet ways set him apart. It was easier here, in the wilderness, to ride alone and leave the judgments of others behind him.

Buffalo Gap was already fading into the horizon, and with it, the betrayal that hung in his memory like a bad storm. He could still see their faces, etched with fear and suspicion, ready to sell him out to save themselves. Only a few months back, they'd pleaded for his help, begged him to stand up against the Oakleys, to fight their fight. And he'd done it, put himself in the line of fire, taking on the very men who'd plagued that town for years. Yet, the minute it looked like the Oakleys might make trouble again, those same folks were ready to hand him over, trading his life for a fleeting moment's peace. He'd stuck around for a while, only because of Alice, but he knew he couldn't stay there. A man could only take so much of that before he got wise.

Nash tightened his hold on the reins, glancing down at the pale buckskin mare. He was mighty careful with her now, if she'd not rattled a shoe loose on a rocky trail his life would have been a lot simpler. And he was careful with her now, keeping her pace easy, letting her take her time on the trails. She was all he had out here— loyal, dependable. She didn't judge him. She didn't care that his blood was half Apache or that he didn't look quite like other men. Out here, alone with her, he could breathe easy.

The sun was dipping low on the horizon, casting a warm, honeyed light over the plains, and Nash guided the mare toward a narrow creek that wound its way through the prairie grass. He dismounted, letting her drink, and crouched by the water's edge, watching his reflection ripple in the shallow water.

He saw his mother's features in his face—the high cheekbones, the dark, steady eyes that gave nothing away. It was a face that could belong in two worlds but never truly belonged to either. The Apache side of him felt strong, like a quiet pulse of pride that he held close to his chest. His mother had taught him to value silence, to walk with the earth, and to know the power of patience. It had served him well, out here. But the white man's blood in him had given him something different—a grit, maybe, or a certain stubbornness that kept him moving forward, even when he didn't know where he was headed.

"Half-breed," the townsfolk muttered when they thought he couldn't hear. And yet, when they needed a gun hand, he was the first one they looked to. But as soon as the danger passed, he was the first they'd throw to the wolves.

He glanced over his shoulder, half-expecting to see the familiar shapes of the people from Buffalo Gap, but there was nothing. Just the prairie, the endless grassland stretching in every direction, open and unmarked. Out here, he didn't have to answer to anyone.

He'd grown used to the solitude, embraced it, even. Sometimes, he'd ride days without seeing another soul, just him and the sky, the sun marking time. Out here, he felt close to his mother's people,

17

felt her spirit in the wind, in the sway of the grass, in the quiet calls of the night. This land had no need for towns or sheriffs, for people who'd sooner turn on a man than stand beside him.

He turned his face up to the sky, feeling the warmth of the sun on his skin. The Apache blood in him made him feel proud of his connection to the land, to the earth itself. His mother had told him stories of his ancestors, warriors who could track a man through the mountains without leaving a trace, men who had learned to survive on the barest of means, men who feared no one and nothing. He carried that with him, a piece of heritage that no town could take from him.

But the white man's blood brought him conflict. It made him think in ways that his mother had called the "white man's trouble"—too much thought and not enough heart. It pulled him in directions that didn't always make sense, that left him feeling restless, haunted by the past and wary of the future.

He stayed by the creek as the shadows lengthened, his thoughts drifting to Buffalo Gap, to the gunfight he'd left behind, and the people who'd turned their backs as quickly as they'd offered their hands. He knew better than to hold a grudge, but the bitterness was hard to shake. They'd wanted a saviour, not a man. And he was done being a saviour.

When the sun sank fully behind the horizon, Nash finally rose, dusting off his hat and adjusting it back on his head. The buckskin mare lifted her head, watching him with dark, patient eyes. He gave her an approving pat, and she lowered her nose to the ground, snuffling softly.

"Guess it's you and me now," he murmured. She whinnied softly, almost as if she understood.

With the town far behind him, he mounted the mare and turned her north, into the deepening night. There were no promises out here, no betrayals, no one to trust or to be disappointed by. Just him, the open plain, and whatever lay on the horizon.

CHAPTER TWO

Nash watched from the cover of the rocks, his sharp gaze tracing the dust clouds that marked the Comanche's relentless pursuit of the cowboy. He'd seen enough chases to know the horse wouldn't hold out, not against the buckskin ponies the Comanche rode, fresh and fierce. And sure enough, within moments, the cowboy's horse began to falter, her steps sluggish, labored, until she staggered to a stop at the edge of the ridge. Nash knew what would come next, and he felt a pang of grim sympathy for the stranger—no one deserved the treatment the Comanche were bound to give him.

From his vantage point, Nash saw the cowboy leap from his exhausted mare and sprint toward a jagged outcrop, clearly hoping the rocks would offer cover. But the Comanche closed in fast, their shouts filling the air, hard and ruthless. They overtook him just as he reached the boulders, surrounding him in a circle that allowed no escape.

Nash's jaw tightened as he watched the scene unfold. The cowboy, his face pale and wild, was beaten down to his knees. The Comanche tore away his guns, his knife, and anything else he had of use. Nash's fingers tightened on the Henry rifle. He could pick off one, maybe two—but three? That would be pushing his luck. Besides, he wasn't in the business of meddling in other men's troubles. He was just passing through, a half-breed stranger in no-man's-land, with no one to answer to and no one he owed a thing to.

But something gnawed at him, something he couldn't ignore.

The cowboy was tossed over his saddle like a sack of grain, his hands bound, head hanging over the side. The Comanche were preparing to leave, satisfied with their capture, when one of them paused, squinting toward the horizon. Nash saw him raise a hand, signaling to the others. They turned in unison, eyes narrowing as they spotted Nash's silhouette, unmistakable on the ridge, the Henry rifle cradled in his arms.

Nash took a steadying breath, feeling the weight of the Henry. He knew he had seconds to decide—to act or to fade back into the hills. Three-to-one odds weren't good, but his gut had already made the call. He raised the Henry and nudged his horse forward, emerging slowly from the shadow of the rocks, his gaze fixed on the three warriors as he approached.

They didn't move at first, their expressions unreadable as they watched him close the distance. He stopped out of the range of any revolvers they had, but they were within the range of his Henry, and they'd know it. Nash had seen the posters in gun stores boasting that the Henry was accurate to a distance of two hundred yards, four times as much as a revolver, but Nash didn't believe it. He knew his rifle was good for a hundred and twenty yards; after that, the bullets strayed, but that didn't matter. At this distance, he could outgun all three of them. Until they closed the gap, that's when his problems would start.

He knew how well they'd be able to ride, and they'd not offer him a target as they approached, dropping round the sides of the buckskins, out of sight. Then, they'd reappear and shoot when they were within range. Another of his mother's sayings crept into his head. "Never underestimate the wind."

Nash pulled his horse to a halt, the Henry ready.

The leader, a tall Comanche with a face painted in streaks of white and red, looked at Nash with an intense gaze, his hand resting on the revolver at his hip. Behind him, the other two shifted uneasily, glancing at each other, unsure if this lone rider posed a real threat. Nash held his ground, his own expression unreadable, a calm mask over the tension coiled within him.

He lifted his hand slowly, gesturing toward the cowboy slung over the saddle. He spoke Comanche, not well, but he knew enough to get his meaning across, "Let him go," he said, his voice low but carrying across the distance. "There's no need for a fight."

The leader's eyes narrowed, and a faint, mocking smile crossed his lips. He responded in his own language. They weren't about to back down, not for one man on his own.

Nash's gaze shifted to the cowboy, slumped, barely conscious, his face bloodied and bruised. Something in that broken, desperate figure stirred a hard determination in him. He raised the Henry, the gun held steady, unwavering, and trained on the leader.

The Comanche leader straightened, recognizing Nash's resolve. He glanced at his two companions, who seemed reluctant but ready, their hands hovering over their weapons. Nash knew that one wrong move would set them off, but he also knew that his next words mattered. He spoke slowly, his voice calm and steady.

"You let him go," he said, his gaze never wavering ", or there's gonna be more blood spilt here than you came looking for."

The leader studied him, his expression unreadable, weighing the stranger's words. Nash could see the calculation in his eyes. For a moment, he thought it might work. But then the leader's expression hardened, his hand moving to his revolver, and Nash's hand tightened on the Henry.

In that charged second, Nash knew he had one shot to make his point clear.

Without breaking eye contact, he lifted the Henry slightly, aiming just past the leader's shoulder, and fired. The bullet struck the saddle of one of their horses, the crack of gunfire echoing across the empty plains. The horse reared, startled, throwing one of the Comanche to the ground, and for a heartbeat, there was nothing but tension, thick as the dust that rose from the shot.

The leader froze his hand still on his revolver. His eyes locked on Nash, who held his ground, the Henry aimed and as steady as stone. Nash's expression was cold and deadly. He wasn't bluffing, and they both knew it.

Slowly, the leader removed his hand from where it had rested on the gun, his jaw clenched with frustration. He barked an order to the others, and with a few terse words, they grudgingly released the cowboy. The cowboy slumped to the ground, his body hitting the dirt with a dull thud, but he was free.

Nash waited, his Henry still steady, as the Comanche gathered their fallen companion and mounted their horses, casting one last look of fury his way. But they didn't linger. One by one, they turned, the leader giving Nash a warning glare before riding off, the dust trailing behind them like a promise of vengeance.

Only when they'd disappeared into the distance did Nash lower the Henry rifle, sliding it back into the saddle holster and nudging his horse forward slowly towards the body laid in the dirt.

Nash approached cautiously, eyes scanning the landscape for any signs of trouble. The man on the ground was struggling, attempting to push himself up with bound hands and feet, every movement hindered by the tight rawhide and fresh bruises that covered his skin. Nash's gaze lingered on the cuts lining the man's cheek, the dried blood on his temple, the marks left by a fight that had clearly gone against him.

Dismounting, Nash kept his hand close to his holster where the Colt .44 waited, ready. His instincts were still on high alert. He moved to the man's side, unsheathing his knife in a smooth motion. Without a word, he bent down, sliding the blade beneath the rawhide at the man's wrists and feet, slicing it away with quick, precise cuts. As the bonds fell loose, Nash saw the deeper bruises hidden beneath, bruises that spoke of a struggle as fierce as it was hopeless.

With the final bond severed, the man sank back, lying flat against the ground as exhaustion and pain pressed down on him like a heavy weight. His breathing was shallow, his chest rising and falling as he surrendered to the release from his restraints. Bruises mottled his face, and his split lip and swollen jaw made even the simplest movement a struggle. Dazed, he looked up at Nash, his breaths coming in short, labored bursts as he tried—and failed—to form words.

Nash watched him closely, noting the man's weakened state. It was clear he posed no threat. Letting his guard down slightly, Nash extended a steady hand toward him.

"Here," Nash said, his voice low but firm. "Let's get you sitting up."

The man hesitated, his eyes searching Nash's face as if unsure whether to trust the outstretched hand. But pain and fatigue won out over caution, and he reached up, clasping Nash's hand with a weak grip. Nash pulled gently, guiding him into a sitting position, steadying him as he swayed slightly, his breath rattling with the effort. Nash's gaze softened as he took in the cuts and bruises scattered across the man's arms and chest, evidence of the brutal encounter. His clothes were ripped, they'd left him with his gun belt, but whatever piece he'd owned had left with the Comanche.

The man gave a slight nod of thanks, but his voice failed him. Nash didn't press him for words, just eased him back against a nearby rock, giving him a moment to catch his breath.

"Take it slow," Nash murmured, keeping his tone steady and calm. He pulled a canteen from his saddlebag, unscrewing the cap before handing it over. "Drink up. No rush."

The man took the canteen, his fingers trembling as he raised it to his lips and drank. The cool water seemed to revive him a little, and for the first time, a hint of relief replaced the strain etched across his face.

The cowboy managed a hoarse whisper. "Thought I was done for," he rasped, wincing as he touched his bruised cheek.

"You nearly were," Nash replied, his tone matter-of-fact. "But don't get too comfortable. They'll be back for you, maybe sooner than you think."

The cowboy nodded, still dazed, but there was a glint of gratitude in his eyes as he met Nash's gaze. "Why'd you help me?" he asked, genuine curiosity mingling with his pain.

Nash shrugged, his expression unreadable. "Couldn't just sit and watch," he said, his voice quiet. "Now let's leave."

Nash glanced over his shoulder, his instincts sharp. The Comanche wouldn't have gone far; they'd regroup, and soon enough, they'd be hunting for the man he'd just freed. Without another word, Nash strode over to the man's weary horse, its coat dusty and its flanks trembling with fatigue. He grabbed the reins and led it back, then bent down, taking hold of the man's arm.

"Let's get you up," he muttered, lifting him with a firm grip. The man grimaced as he was hoisted onto the saddle, slumping forward, his body swaying slightly from weakness. Some distance away, caught in the whisps of sagebrush, was the man's hat; Nash retrieved it and returned it to its owner.

Nash ensured he was as steady as possible before taking hold of the reins. They couldn't afford to linger. With a final look at the spot where the Comanche had caught up with the man, Nash turned, leading the horse and its weary rider away.

CHAPTER THREE

Nash led them to the ridge crest, where the land fell away into the vast, open plains below. It was the kind of vantage point that made a man feel powerful and small, the entire world stretching out around them in dusty blues and golds beneath the deepening evening sky. Here, he'd have a clear line of sight in every direction—a spot where no one could approach unseen. It was a place that gave them breathing room and a moment's safety, at least for now.

He reined in the horses and set up a modest camp around his battered companion. First, he unsaddled the man's horse, noticing the sweat-darkened spots along its back. The horse had been pushed hard, and its sides heaved as it finally rested. Nash gave it a few gentle pats, his touch calming as he led it to a patch of buffalo grass and tied it off next to his own mare, giving both horses a chance to graze and recover.

When the horses were settled, Nash turned back toward the man lying on the ground. He still looked dazed, his face shadowed by the lingering bruises from the fight. Nash crouched down beside him, watching him quietly for a moment.

"How you feelin'?" Nash asked, his voice low, not expecting much of a response.

The man's lips twitched in what looked for a second like a smirk, but it was more than likely a grimace of pain. "Better than I was," he managed, his voice rough, "but that's not saying much."

Nash let out a faint chuckle. "Reckon, you've seen better days," he replied. He took his canteen and handed it over, watching as the man took a slow, careful sip before he handed it back to Nash.

They sat in silence for a while, the quiet around them punctuated by the soft snorts and shuffling of the horses. Nash pulled a small fire together to offer warmth and keep away the chill that crept in as the sun dipped below the horizon.

"You got a name?" Nash asked eventually, watching the stranger over the tiny flicker of the fire.

"Cain," the man muttered, his gaze distant. "Matt Cain."

Nash nodded, filing it away as he studied Cain's face. Something about the man's eyes was sharp and calculating despite his battered state, a glint that made Nash wonder just what kind of trouble he'd gotten himself into to warrant such a brutal chase by the Comanche.

"And you?" Can asked through his bruised lips.

"Nash," Nash replied, sounding a little more blunt than he'd meant it to be.

Cain nodded and said, "Thank you, Nash. I can't say how much I appreciate you stopping."

Cain was about the same height as Nash, with the same lean muscular build that spoke of years of rugged survival. His hair was a dark, chestnut brown, tangled and falling just past his ears, now matted with blood that had leaked from cuts on his head. His face was angular, with high cheekbones and a strong, square jaw that hinted at both resilience and stubbornness. His skin, deeply tanned from the relentless sun, bore the scars and lines of a man who's seen more than his share of battles. Cain's piercing grey eyes were still sharp and observant despite the rough handling he'd recently received, and, propped up on one elbow, his clothes in tatters, his body beaten, he still exuded a calm, calculating confidence.

"Well, Cain," Nash said, his voice steady as he tossed a couple of sticks onto the fire, the flames crackling softly. "I'd say you're lucky I found you when I did. But if there are more folks on your trail, it'd be good to know about it now, not when they're breathing down our necks." Nash, his face expressionless, asked, "What'd you do to rile them Comanche up that much?"

Cain shifted, grimacing as he adjusted his position. He looked up at Nash, his expression hard to read, a mix of gratitude and caution lingering in his eyes. He let out a weary sigh. "They were after whatever they could get from me. I Just... crossed paths with 'em at the wrong time. Guess they don't like strangers."

"Strangers they tie up and beat near half to death?" Nash's voice was low, unimpressed. "That wasn't just a bad encounter. Looked to me like they had a real purpose in mind."

Nash narrowed his eyes, watching Cain closely as he handed the canteen back to him,

"Thank you," Cain said, accepting the canteen. "It's just the way things go, I guess. When a man has a few things worth taking, there's always someone who thinks they've got a right to it."

His words trailed off, leaving enough unspoken to make Nash wonder if there was more to the story than Cain was letting on. It wasn't exactly usual for the Comanche to take a prisoner. If they'd wanted the man's belongings, they'd have taken them and left him for dead, or they'd have left him alone on the plains without a canteen or his horse, which pretty much amounted to the same thing.

"Well," Nash said after a pause, "whatever the reason, we'll be keeping a close watch tonight. And come dawn, we'll be moving quick." He fixed Cain with a steady look. "I didn't stick my neck out just to end up another target."

Cain met his gaze, his mouth pulling into a faint, tired smile. "Can't argue with that," he murmured, nodding slightly. "I owe you, Nash. You didn't have to help me. But I'll make sure you don't regret it."

Nash let his gaze linger on Cain, then turned his attention back to the fire, watching the flames lick the dry wood, casting shadows around their makeshift camp. He'd have to trust his instincts this time—he didn't know what Cain was hiding, but he'd be ready if the man's troubles decided to follow them through the night. Nash's gaze held steady on him for a moment longer before he looked away, out into the sprawling night beyond the ridge. He knew better than to ask too many questions just yet. Cain would either trust him or he wouldn't, and Nash wasn't keen to be caught up in another man's quarrels—at least, not until he knew which side he stood on. For now, he'd keep watch, and come morning, he'd decide which trail to take, trusting his instincts to steer him in the right direction as they usually did.

Nash stirred from a fitful sleep, the remnants of his mother's voice still clinging to his mind. She'd been scolding him, her familiar voice sharp and disappointed, chastising him for getting mixed up in trouble that wasn't his.

"What were you thinking, boy?" she'd said, arms crossed, a familiar crease in her brow. "You've got enough on your plate without hauling around stray trouble." He could practically see her shaking her head at him, her expression softened only by a trace of concern beneath the scolding.

When dawn finally crept over the horizon, Nash rubbed his eyes, groggy and restless, and went about preparing a small fire. He dug out his battered coffee pot, filling it with water and coffee grounds, letting the earthy aroma settle his mind as it brewed. He poured a tin mug and handed it to Cain, who accepted it gratefully, his eyes lighting up at the first sip.

Cain looked up from his cup, offering Nash a grateful nod. "This... is some damn good coffee. Haven't had anything like this in a while," he murmured, cradling the mug as if it were a treasure. After a long sip, he glanced over, his voice softer. "I don't know what I would've done if you hadn't come along, Nash. I reckon I owe you more than just thanks. And when we get to a town, I'm going to repay your kindness."

Nash shrugged, sipping his coffee and letting the warmth wake him fully. "Did what anyone would do," he replied, though he wasn't entirely sure that was true. His mother's imagined voice was still there, a wisp of reproach in the back of his mind.

Cain looked at him, that glint of gratitude still bright in his tired eyes. "Well, doesn't mean it's nothing," he said. They sat in comfortable silence, the dawn quiet around them, each of them savoring the coffee.

CHAPTER FOUR

They set off at a slow pace, the silence between them stretching long and thick, broken only by the occasional crunch of their horses' hooves against the sunbaked dirt. Nash kept his gaze forward, his mind turning over the encounter, trying to piece together the strange puzzle of Matt Cain. His unease wasn't just from Cain's demeanor—it was the whole setup, the way the Comanche had gone after him, so determined, so intent. Nash had seen vendettas before, but something about this felt different, darker. And why did they want to take him with them? That was a puzzle in itself.

After a while, Cain cleared his throat, breaking the silence. "I'm guessin' a man like you doesn't settle much," he said, his tone casual, but Nash could feel the probing in the words.

Nash shrugged, his face unreadable. "I don't have a reason to settle anywhere."

"Fair enough," Cain replied, nodding slowly. He paused, studying Nash's face. "Though I've gotta say, you don't strike me as the type to intervene in other folks' problems. What made you step in back there?"

Nash kept his eyes on the trail. "Figured it wasn't my place to stand by and watch a man get taken down by three others, whether they had cause or not." He cast Cain a sidelong look. "Maybe you got yourself in that mess for a reason."

Cain's mouth twisted in a half-smile, though it didn't reach his eyes. "Maybe I'm just unlucky."

"Unlucky doesn't make three Comanche risk a pursuit that far out," Nash replied, his voice low and even. "Unlucky gets a man shot in a skirmish, maybe. But that?" He shook his head, his tone flat. "That was something else. And why did they want to take you with them?"

"That I can't answer, Nash. I don't know what's in a Comanche's mind," Cain said, then added. "Like you, I was alone on the trail; I saw them coming towards me, and before I could make an escape, they'd caught up."

Nash nodded, but his expression told the other man he wasn't entirely convinced.

Cain said nothing more, his gaze falling to the ground as they rode on. Nash didn't press further; he'd learned over the years that people revealed themselves in their own time and sometimes not at all. The trail stretched out before them, long and dusty, the horizon wavering in the heat. The Comanche would be behind them by now, but Nash couldn't shake the sense that they weren't finished. Men with a purpose didn't give up so easily, and there was a good chance they'd see them again.

As they rode, Nash's mind returned to Buffalo Gap, the way folks there turned against him when it suited them, and the familiar feeling of mistrust stirred. Maybe he should have left Cain to his fate, let the man handle his own problems. But now he was committed, and he'd see it through—at least as far as the next town. Then he could leave the man; he'd done his duty, and, more in fact, he would head out on his own again.

The shadows were stretched and long when Nash finally spoke, his voice quiet but firm. "If we're ridin' together, Cain, there's one thing you oughta know."

Cain looked over, his expression unreadable. "And what's that?"
Nash's gaze was steady, his tone flat. "I'm not in the business of babysitting, nor do I plan to start. If the trouble you've got comes followin' us to Abilene, don't expect me to stick around to see how it ends."

Cain's lips twitched into a humorless smile. "Fair enough, Nash. I wouldn't expect any different." He tipped his hat in a mock salute, his eyes glinting with something almost like respect. "Here's to an easy ride."

Nash just nodded, his face stony as they continued down the trail, his mind restless. For better or worse, he was tied to Cain for the moment, but if his instincts were right, he had a feeling their path would only get rougher from here on out.

As Nash and Cain rode deeper into the rugged, twisting landscape, the day was clear and unbroken. The sun cast stark shadows across the canyon walls, throwing jagged rock and dry brush into sharp relief. They'd been riding in silence for hours, their horses kicking up dust along the narrow, winding trail, when Nash's gut tensed with an unease he couldn't ignore.

There was a stillness here that didn't sit right, an unnatural quiet that set Nash's senses on edge. He glanced at Cain, who seemed perfectly calm, his eyes scanning the canyon walls with a practiced detachment. Something in Cain's demeanor unsettled Nash, something too careful, too measured.

That feeling, the quiet, made Nash reach for his Colt just as a shadow flitted across a ridge above them. Without warning, a shot cracked through the air, the echo ricocheting off the canyon walls like a thunderclap. Nash jerked his reins, his horse rearing as another shot rang out, splintering the rock inches from his head. He spurred the horse forward, dodging for cover behind a jagged outcrop, his heart hammering.

More shots exploded, raining down like hailstones. Nash gritted his teeth, his mind racing as he tried to pinpoint their attackers. At least three of them, he guessed, were hidden among the rocks above them. He looked around for Cain, who had wheeled his horse into the narrow shelter of a rock ledge just behind him, his face set with a hard focus.

Cain's eyes were fixed on the ridge where one of the shooters had exposed himself, reloading. Cain's voice was low but urgent. "Throw me your Colt, I got a clear shot."

Nash hesitated, his grip tightened around the Colt's handle. He didn't like the idea of handing over his gun, especially to a man he barely knew. For a moment, he weighed his options, considering the risk. But the edge in Cain's voice—and the steady way he kept his eyes on the target—pushed him past his reluctance.

With a small grunt of resignation, Nash tossed the Colt to Cain, who caught it with steady hands. Without missing a beat, Cain took aim, his movements quick but precise. His jaw set, his gaze lined up, and he squeezed the trigger.

The shot rang out, echoing against the ridge, and a second later, Nash heard the man cry out and tumble from the ledge, disappearing in a cloud of dust. Cain had hit his mark cleanly, not a moment of hesitation in the shot. He handed the Colt back to Nash, a small, satisfied grin tugging at the corner of his mouth.

Cain grinned back at Nash.

"Get down!" Nash shouted, half expecting Cain to follow him into cover.

But Cain stayed upright, his movements sure, each shot deliberate. He seemed to sense where the attackers would emerge, his focus never wavering. The gun found its mark with a ruthless efficiency that made Nash's skin crawl. Cain fought with an almost eerie detachment, like a man who'd done this more times than he could count.

Nash darted out, returning fire when he could, the canyon walls swallowing the noise as they volleyed shot for shot. Another man fell, clutching his shoulder, his rifle clattering against the rocks. Cain was already moving, advancing with a brutal precision that made Nash pause, taken aback by the transformation in his companion.

Nash had the Henry free of the saddle holster, but from where he was he couldn't see any of the attackers, it was only Cain behind him who had a view of the attackers above them.

The Colt in Cain's hand clicked on an empty chamber.

Cain turned to Nash. "Throw me your other Colt and reload this one."

It wasn't a request. It was an order, and a second later, Nash was catching the empty Colt from the air tossed to him by Cain. Setting the Henry against the canyon wall, he pulled his other Colt from the holster and threw it to Cain. Then, with steady hands, he began plugging cartridges into the empty Colt. His eyes were on the gun he was loading, and he heard the shots from his gun in Cain's hand reverberate around the canyon. From above them came another choked cry as another bullet found its mark.

Cain fired the last shot from the Colt and turned back to Nash grinning he said. "Catch. One to go."

Nash threw the loaded Colt towards him and caught the empty one; pressing the chamber open, he began sliding in another set of rounds. Before he'd finished reloading the gun, Cain had stepped swiftly from the cover of the rocks and fired three shots in quick succession before stepping back behind the rocks.

Nash loaded the last round, snapped the chamber shut and listened. The canyon had suddenly fallen into an uneasy silence, the air thick with the smell of gunpowder and dust. Cain stepped from his cover, the revolver still raised, his eyes darting to each corner of the canyon, calm as ever, there was no fear in his eyes. No sign of rattled nerves, no indication that he'd been in any real danger. He glanced over at Nash, his expression unreadable.

"That'll be all of 'em?" Cain said, turning to Nash.

Nash's grip tightened on his revolver as he stared at the man. "Reckon so," he replied, the words coming slow, measured. "Didn't realize I was travelin' with a gunslinger."

Cain gave a faint shrug, slipping Nash's revolver back into his own holster. "Not my first scrape," he said, his tone casual, almost dismissive. He began to walk back to his horse as if he hadn't just taken down three armed men without so much as breaking a sweat.

"Seems like a lot more than that," Nash pressed, watching Cain with a wary gaze. "That sort of calm, the way you fought—that don't come easy. Least, not without a reason."

Cain paused, his eyes narrowing ever so slightly. "You got questions, Nash?" His voice was low, almost too calm, and for a brief moment, Nash thought he saw something flicker in Cain's gaze— something dark, something dangerous.

Nash studied him, weighing his words. "Yeah, reckon I do," he replied slowly. "Seems to me you handled yourself a little too well back there. And those men weren't just lookin' for any cowboy. They were lookin' for someone like you."

Cain's lips twitched, but his expression remained impassive. "You saved me from the Comanche, Nash. Guess I didn't think you'd get curious about what brought them to me." He mounted his horse, his movements smooth despite the tension in the air and injuries he'd recently suffered.

Nash hesitated, his own mind racing. He'd learned a long time ago to trust his instincts, and right now, they were screaming at him to keep his distance. Cain had too many secrets, secrets that seemed to follow him like a shadow, and Nash wasn't interested in getting tangled in another man's troubles.

"You didn't answer my question," Nash pressed, his voice steady but his gaze sharp.

Cain looked down at him, his face shadowed. "Maybe that's because you don't want the answer." He gave Nash a stern look, the tension between them palpable. "Maybe you're better off thinkin' of me as just a man who was in the wrong place at the wrong time."

Nash held his gaze, the silence stretching between them, thick as molasses. He didn't like the way Cain's words hung in the air, didn't like the feeling gnawing at the edge of his mind that he'd made a mistake by letting this man tag along. Sure, he'd freed him from the Comanche, but something told him that Cain was no ordinary prisoner.

Nash dropped his gaze to the Colt that was in Cain's holster, it was one of his Colts. "I'll take my piece back now."

Cain smiled and patted the holster. "I think she's better off with me now, don't you? Abilene's still a ways off," he said, his voice flat. "Let's get movin'."

Before Nash could reply, Cain mounted his horse and urged her forward. Nash couldn't shake the feeling that he was heading toward a storm, one he might not be able to escape. But for now, he'd keep riding. And he'd keep a close eye on Matt Cain – what choice did he have? Cain alone had been one thing, but now Cain armed was quite another, and Nash was pretty sure he wouldn't willingly part with the Colt.

That night, the fire crackled between them, throwing flickers of warm light between them. of the canyon. He glanced at Cain across the flames, still feeling the rush of their encounter, the surge of adrenaline that hadn't entirely faded.

"I didn't realize you were a gunslinger," Nash said, breaking the silence.

Cain looked over, a grin playing on his lips. "You're not too bad yourself," he replied. "You just lack confidence. The more you have of it, the faster you get, the more accurate."

Nash nodded as if he could absorb that confidence through sheer agreement. "It's just practice, I guess."

Cain's grin widened, and suddenly, he stood, dusting off his hands. "Then get up. Come on, draw against me—fast as you can."

Nash froze, glancing down at his gun holstered against his thigh. "Here?" he asked, eyes widening in surprise.

Cain just chuckled, motioning him up with a wave of his hand. "Yes, here. Don't worry. I'm not aiming to hit you. It's just practice like you said. Get up."

Cain took the Colt from the holster, emptied the rounds into his hand, and pocketed them. Nash, breathing a little easier, did the same. Hesitantly, Nash rose, brushing the dust off his pants as he squared up opposite Cain. His heart started to race, and his hand hovered over his gun, fingers twitching.

"Ready?" Cain asked, his tone easy but his eyes sharp.

Nash nodded, and before he could think twice, his hand went for his gun, but Cain was faster—effortlessly faster. By the time Nash's hand gripped his weapon, Cain's was already leveled at him, a playful gleam in his eyes.

Again and again, they tried. Each time Nash's hand went for his gun, Cain was already there, steady and calm. Frustration started to creep in, but Cain was patient, even as he outdrew Nash every single time. As Nash tried to outdraw Cain he got worse, twice catching the Colt on the top of the holster and failing to draw her cleanly from the leather. Nash heard his mother's words in his head, admonishing him for his lack of calm. Silently he acknowledged her and dropped the Colt back into the holster.

"It's because it's natural to me," Cain explained, finally holstering his weapon and folding his arms. "I've done it so often, the gun feels like a part of my body. I don't think about drawing—I just do it. It's all in the practice. You have to stop thinking and let your instincts take over. Don't feel bad, Nash. You're fast, real fast, but I got the edge, and you can get it to "

Nash blew out a breath, nodding. "So how do I do that?"

Cain stepped closer, reaching for Nash's hand and adjusting his grip on the weapon. "First off, relax. Don't overthink it. Feel the weight of the gun, let your body get used to it." He demonstrated, hand sliding over the holster, moving with a fluid grace that made the movement seem deceptively simple.

"Start slow," Cain said, his voice low and steady. "You draw, put it back, draw again. Over and over. Until it's in your bones."

Nash followed his lead, drawing in a steady rhythm, his hand getting a little surer each time. Cain circled him, watching closely, occasionally nudging his stance or correcting his grip.

"Good," Cain murmured, nodding in approval. "The more you do it, the faster you'll get. Then, you won't even have to think about it one day. Your piece will be in your hand when you need it."

Nash met Cain's gaze, a flicker of gratitude in his eyes. "Thanks. I'm... I'm getting there, I think."

Cain's smile softened, and he clapped Nash on the shoulder. "You've got the spark, Nash. Now, just keep at it. One day, you might even outdraw me."

They both chuckled, settling back down by the fire as the desert night deepened, the warmth of Cain's words lingering long after the flames had dimmed. Cain had shared his skill willingly, taking the time to tell Nash where he was going wrong, correcting his grip, improving his stance, helping him. Maybe he could learn from the man. That was a good thing, surely?

His head pillowed on his saddle, eyes finally closed to the stars above, another voice chided him.

"Cain's just showing you that there's no way you can outgun him and get your piece back."

Nash closed his eyes a little tighter, he didn't want to listen to that voice, not right now.

CHAPTER FIVE

They set off just after sunrise; Nash and Cain rode side by side, the day's first light casting long shadows across the dusty trail. The ambush in the canyon lingered in Nash's mind, the memory of Cain's sharp, deliberate moves replaying itself. He wanted to trust Cain, to believe the man had just been a victim of bad luck—but something didn't sit right.

After a stretch of silence, Nash stopped his horse, turning to face Cain. "Think it's time we had a talk," he said, his voice calm but resolute.

Cain, who'd been scanning the horizon, looked over with a faint smile. "About what?"

"About that ambush." Nash's eyes narrowed, but his gaze showed a trace of understanding. "Men don't come gunnin' for just anyone like that. And you don't fight like you did without a story behind it."

Cain's smile faded, and a guarded look crept over his face, his shoulders tensing. "I told you, Nash—wrong place, wrong time."

Nash shook his head, his tone even but unyielding. "Doesn't sit right. You've got too many shadows tailing you for this to be a one-off. So, why don't you give me the truth, Cain? What brought those men after you?"

Cain sighed, running a hand over his jaw as if weighing how much to say. "Alright," he muttered, glancing at Nash with a flicker of resigned amusement. "But it ain't gonna make you sleep any easier."

"Try me."

Cain shifted in the saddle, his gaze distant as he spoke. "Used to run in... questionable circles. It started with gambling, you know? Make a few bad bets, owed a few of the wrong people, and suddenly you're keeping company with folks who'd sooner shoot than shake hands."

Nash listened, his expression softening but his focus unbroken. "Go on."

Cain's jaw tightened, his voice dropping. "I made some enemies—debts I couldn't pay, partners I crossed when things got tight. There's a line of folks who wouldn't mind seeing me in the ground. Those men back there?" He paused a flicker of regret in his eyes. "Just the latest in a long line."

Nash gave a slow nod, taking it in, his gaze steady. "Thanks for leveling with me."

Cain met his eyes, his expression softened by a rare trace of gratitude. "Well, I owe you that much."

Nash studied him, the silence thickening as he mulled over Cain's words. Something in his story rang true, but there was an emptiness and a hollow quality. "If it's just some gambling debts and a few bad partners, why were the Comanche after you?"

Cain leaned back in his saddle, his gaze drifting to the horizon as if seeing something far off, something buried in memory.

"Look, Nash," he started, a faint grimace crossing his face, "that business with the Comanche... that was just me bein' in the wrong place at the wrong time. I figure they were already riled up over somethin' else—someone else, even—long before I crossed their path."

Nash listened quietly, his curiosity piqued, while Cain kept his eyes fixed on the distant plains as if the land itself held the weight of his story.

"I was ridin' through their territory, just keepin' to myself, when I saw the first signs." Cain's voice grew quieter, almost thoughtful. "Smoke, fires in the distance, you know? Tension in the air. I kept my head down, but it wasn't long before they found me."

He paused, a shadow flickering in his eyes as he recalled the encounter. "They didn't waste time on questions. I could tell right off they were angry like somethin' had already put their blood up. Maybe some settler crossed a line; maybe some other fool got on their wrong side. Either way, they saw me, and that was enough."

Nash frowned, watching Cain closely. "So, they just... took it out on you?"

Cain nodded slowly. "Yep. Didn't matter who I was or what I was doin'. All they saw was someone who didn't belong. I tried talkin' 'em down, but they weren't hearin' it. Reckon they'd already made up their minds by then."

Nash nodded, taking it in, understanding more of the man's guarded expression and quiet toughness. "That's rough," he said, his tone laced with respect. "Wrong place, wrong time."

Cain gave him a brief, weary smile. "Story of my life," he muttered.

Cain shifted in his saddle, a faint smirk tugging at the corner of his mouth as he looked at Nash. "You know, that Comanche business wasn't the only time trouble found me without me lookin' for it. A couple of months back, I was just passing through this town, figured I'd stop in the saloon for a quick drink to break up the ride."

He paused, his smirk widening, the memory dancing in his eyes. "No sooner do I sit down than some fella across the room starts mouthing off to a local tough. Next thing I know, guns are drawn, fists are flyin', and half the place is duckin' for cover."

Nash chuckled, recognizing the chaotic scene all too well, but he kept quiet, listening.

Cain continued, "I didn't want any part of it. I kept my head down and tried to mind my own business, but before I knew it, someone knocked over my table, and one of those fools thought I was on the other side. I tried talkin' sense, but it's hard to reason with a man when he's holdin' a broken bottle and shoutin' about his pride."

"So what happened?" Nash asked, unable to hide a bit of amusement.

"Well," Cain said, leaning forward, "I tried to slip out before things got worse, but that's when the sheriff and his boys came bustin' in, ready to arrest anyone with a face they didn't recognize. All I could do was high-tail it out of there before they threw me in a cell for good measure. Spent the night dodgin' their patrols, waitin' for a chance to get clear."

Nash's face softened, an understanding nod replacing his usual caution. "Sounds like Buffalo Gap," he said, a wry grin spreading across his face. "I've had my own share of 'wrong place, wrong time' moments myself. Got tangled up in a mess just like that, and no one believed I wasn't in on it."

Cain looked at him, a faint glint of appreciation in his eye. "Yeah, it's a hard tale to swallow unless you've been there yourself. Sometimes folks don't need much reason to assume the worst."

Nash gave a slow nod, his doubts about Cain starting to ease. He could see the familiar pattern of a man who'd had to dodge trouble simply for passing through, a man whose reputation was a bit more complicated than he let on.

"Well, here's to leavin' trouble behind us for a change," Nash said, tipping his hat slightly.

Cain nodded in agreement, his expression softening. "I'll drink to that, and I sure owe you a whiskey or two."

The sky was fading to dusk as Nash and Cain made a small camp, setting up near a cluster of low rocks to break the wind. The fire crackled warmly, casting a soft glow on the landscape around them as they sat side by side, each lost in their thoughts for a while.

After a bit, Cain glanced at Nash, a spark of mischief in his eyes. "Come on, Nash, let's practice your draw," Cain said, his voice casual but his gaze keen. "You're not bad. Where did you learn? Your Pa? Brother, maybe?"

Nash shrugged, poking at the fire with a stick. "Ain't much of a gunslinger. I know how to handle myself, but I've never had a proper teacher."

Cain raised an eyebrow, tilting his head. "Well, maybe it's time you had one. Stand up. Let's get some more time in."

Nash hesitated, but something in Cain's steady, almost brotherly gaze made him give in. He rose to his feet, his hand resting on his holster as he looked at Cain for guidance.

"Alright," Cain said, getting up and studying Nash's stance. "Now, relax a bit. You're still too stiff. What did I tell you yesterday—you'll miss your shot if you're tensed up like that. Bend your knees a little but try and keep your shoulders loose."

Nash adjusted, feeling a little self-conscious but strangely grateful for the attention. Cain stepped closer, adjusting Nash's hand placement and the angle of his stance, his movements sure and practiced.

"Better," Cain murmured, nodding approvingly. "Now, on my count, go for the draw. Don't think too hard about it; let it come naturally. Remember what I said: it's just a part of you."

Nash took a steadying breath, waiting for Cain's cue.

"Three... two... one... draw!"

Cain didn't draw the Colt from his gunbelt this time; instead, he just clapped. "Well done. That's better. It's more fluid. Just keep that going."

Nash's hand moved again, and drew the Colt for a second time.

Cain chuckled, shaking his head.

"Not bad for a start," he said, giving Nash a pat on the back. "But don't pull your shoulder forward like that—you'll throw your aim off. Let's try it again."

They practiced together, the rhythm becoming smoother with each draw. Cain offered quiet encouragement and gentle corrections, his tone relaxed, almost friendly. Nash hadn't felt this kind of camaraderie in a long time. He'd known few men who would bother to teach him like this, and even fewer who had the patience for it. With each draw, he felt a bit more confident, his stance a bit more balanced.

Cain stepped back, watching as Nash executed another draw, this one much cleaner, his aim steady.

"There you go," Cain said, his voice carrying a hint of pride. "You keep that up, and you'll be one hell of a shot."

Nash looked at him, a rare grin tugging at his mouth. "I reckon I might, with a teacher like you."

As they leaned back by the fire, the stars glittering above, Cain let out a small chuckle, shaking his head as if at some distant memory.

"What's funny?" Nash asked, his curiosity piqued.

Cain grinned, rubbing his jaw. "Ah, just thinkin' about a time I was workin' as a hand on a cattle drive. Not somethin' I talk about often, but..." He laughed again. "There's this one story that gets me every time."

Nash leaned forward, intrigued. He hadn't known Cain to laugh much, and seeing this side of him was oddly reassuring. "Let's hear it, then."

Cain shook his head, still grinning. "Alright, alright. So, we were about halfway through the drive, somewhere out near Pecos, when we realized one of the young steers had taken a particular shine to me. I'd walk by, and it'd follow me like a dog, just trottin' along, wouldn't leave my side. The boys called him 'Little Cain,' on account of him stickin' to me like glue."

Nash laughed, picturing the scene. "Didn't mind the company, I reckon?"

"Oh, I didn't mind at first," Cain admitted, "but it got worse. See, whenever I'd go off to grab a bite or catch some sleep, that dang steer would bleat loud enough to wake the dead if he couldn't see me. Boss was about ready to shoot it, thinkin' I'd put some kind of spell on the poor creature."

Nash chuckled, shaking his head. "You must've been some sight, tryin' to sneak away from a love-struck steer."

"You're tellin' me. I thought I'd finally lost him one night when we stopped at a town for supplies. But no, next thing I know, I'm in the saloon, mindin' my own business, when the place erupts in shouts. Turn around, and there's Little Cain in the doorway, lookin' around like he'd come to fetch me."

Nash burst out laughing, the image of a lone steer barging into a saloon too funny to resist. "I can't believe it!"

Cain nodded, his own laughter joining Nash's. "Neither could anyone else. Bartender tried to chase him out, but Little Cain just stood his ground like he owned the place. I had to walk him out myself, all the way back to camp, with everyone watchin' and hootin' like I was escortin' some highborn lady."

They both laughed, the sound echoing across the quiet night, the firelight flickering over their faces. Nash relaxed more, the story chipping away at his lingering doubts. There was something real and easy in Cain's voice, a side of him that Nash hadn't seen until now.

"Seems you've got a knack for drawin' attention, one way or another," Nash teased.

Cain gave a rueful nod, his grin lingering. "Maybe so. But every now and then, it makes for a good story. Least I didn't end up with Little Cain as a permanent shadow."

Nash chuckled, still picturing the ridiculous scene. "You ever think about wranglin' steers instead of trouble?"

Cain smirked. "Ah, trouble just has a way of findin' me. But maybe I oughta take it as a sign to stick to the cattle instead."

The conversation eased into a comfortable silence, and Nash leaned back, feeling a warmth settle in his chest. He realized he genuinely enjoyed hearing Cain's stories, and for the first time, he thought that maybe—just maybe—there was more to the man than shadows and secrets. They settled back by the fire, the silence between them broken only by the crackling flames and the occasional murmur from Cain, sharing stories of close calls and near misses. Nash felt the nagging doubts still, but they were quieter now, softened by the simple pleasure of company he didn't know he'd been missing.

As the stars emerged, they both leaned back, staring up at the sky, a strange and unexpected trust slowly growing between them.

CHAPTER SIX

The frontier town was little more than a scattering of buildings on either side of a single dusty street. A general store, a livery, a saloon with sagging doors, and a small jail made up the bulk of it, but to Nash, it was enough to stock up on supplies and maybe hear some news.

The sun was just starting to dip low over the little town, casting long shadows across the dusty main street, and Nash could feel the townsfolks eyes on him. Men, women, even a couple of kids—all watching him as he passed, their glances sharp with suspicion and more than a little fear. He and Cain rode in quietly, the heat from the late afternoon sun weighing on their shoulders. Cain wasted no time dismounting, muttering something about needing to "see a man about a horse", and wandering off toward the saloon, leaving his horse at the small hitching rail outside. Nash watched him go and headed to the store.

The town's quiet felt unnatural. Only a few townsfolk lingered outside, and they fell silent as Nash passed. The shop was small and dimly lit, smelling of tobacco, gun oil, and stale biscuits. As he stepped inside, the bell above the door jangled, announcing his presence.

The shopkeeper, a grizzled older man with a thin mustache and wire-rimmed glasses, nodded and looked up from his ledger. Nash began browsing the shelves, grabbing a few essentials: dried beef, coffee, and a fresh box of cartridges.

As he gathered his supplies, he caught snatches of conversation from a few men in the corner, their voices low and wary. At first, he thought it was just the usual town gossip, but then he heard something that made him pause.

"Heard tell he's ridin' through with a stranger," one of the men muttered. "Looks mighty like that fella Cain. You know, the one with that reward on his head."

Nash felt his pulse quicken. He forced himself to remain calm, to look as if he hadn't heard a thing. The news that there was a price on Cain's head was not what he wanted to hear.

"If it's him, he's got some gall comin' through here," another man replied, his voice tight with distrust. "What's he expectin'? Some kinda safe harbor?"

The first man snorted. "Damn fool, if you ask me. He knows his name carries a price. Could be a bounty hunter here any minute."

Nash felt the eyes of the men shift his way as if they suddenly remembered they weren't alone. He focused on the shelves, pretending to be engrossed in a row of tins, but he could feel the weight of their stares. Every fiber in his body told him to leave, to get out of that store and find Cain before things turned ugly.

"Afternoon, stranger," one of the men called out, a hint of challenge in his voice. Nash looked up, meeting his eyes. The man was broad-shouldered, his face weathered by sun and wind, and his hand rested loosely on the butt of his gun.

"Afternoon," Nash replied evenly, his tone neutral.

"Lookin' for anything particular?" the man asked, his eyes narrowing. He didn't smile, and his hand stayed where it was, fingers tracing the curve of his revolver's handle.

"Just passin' through," Nash replied, keeping his voice calm, the lie resting heavily on his tongue. "Pickin' up some supplies."

The man's gaze lingered, sizing him up. He seemed to hesitate momentarily as if weighing whether to push further, but eventually, he gave a slow nod.

"Can't be too careful out here," he said. "Lots of... questionable folks passin' through these parts. You get my drift?"

Nash met his stare, his hand steady as he held his purchases. "I get it," he replied coolly. "But I'm not lookin' for trouble."

The man's mouth twitched in what might have been a smirk. "Well, trouble's got a way of finding folks, whether they're lookin' for it or not."

With that, he tipped his hat slightly, his gaze lingering before he turned back to his companions. Nash paid for his supplies quickly, eager to leave the oppressive air of the store.

He'd been getting stares since he rode in, but now, standing outside the store, the weight of those looks felt different. They weren't just curious glances, they were wary, measuring, like they were sizing him up.

Nash could see a couple of men lingering near the edge of the street, their postures casual, but their eyes fixed on him with thinly veiled hostility. One of them leaned over to his companion, murmuring something behind the brim of his hat, and they both chuckled low. Nash didn't need to hear the words to know their thoughts. Word travelled fast in a place like this, Cain had a price on his head and by association, it wouldn't be a big leap for them to start assuming Nash was part of Cain's crimes.

Everything in him wanted to ride off, leave this place, and leave Cain to whatever trouble was haunting him. But he wasn't blind to the situation. Alone, he'd be an easy target for anyone with a gun and a taste for bounty money. With Cain, he at least had someone who could watch his back while they got away from the town.

As if on cue, one of the men near the street muttered loud enough for Nash to catch: "Looks like Cain picked up a partner."

Nash felt his jaw tighten, but he didn't react, keeping his eyes fixed on his horse as he tightened the cinch and mounted up. He could feel the prickle of doubt, his own reluctance gnawing at him, but the hard fact was this—out here, with bounty hunters likely on Cain's trail, he was safer with the man than without. At least for now.

He caught sight of Cain slipping out of the saloon.

"Cain," Nash called out, his voice low. "Where the hell have you been?" Nash demanded, his tone edged with frustration.

Cain shrugged, grinning. "Just takin' care of some business."

"Seems like folks in town recognize you," Nash said, his voice a low rumble.

"Talkin' about a bounty. Seems you got more than just a few debts after all."

Cain's expression hardened, his jaw setting as he looked away, clearly uncomfortable under Nash's scrutiny. "I told you, Nash," he replied, his voice barely more than a growl. "I got a past. So do you."

Nash's gaze didn't waver, his patience thinning with every evasive answer. "A man's past don't bring bounty hunters down on him for nothin'."

Cain's eyes darkened, and for a brief moment, Nash saw something cold and dangerous flicker there, something that made him wonder just how much of a mistake he'd made by helping this man. But Cain quickly looked away, pulling his hat lower over his eyes.

"Believe what you want," he muttered, his voice flat. "But unless you're plannin' on turnin' me in, I suggest we get the hell outta here before things get any hotter."

Cain swung up onto his horse, casting a glance at Nash, his eyes glinting with something close to amusement. "Ready?" he asked, his voice low.

Nash gave a curt nod, not meeting Cain's gaze. "Let's get moving."

As they rode out of town, the last rays of sunlight cast long shadows over the dusty street, bathing the worn facades of buildings in an amber glow. Nash's eyes drifted to the old, rundown sheriff's office as they passed, its weathered wood creaking in the breeze, windows smudged and cracked. Just outside, a handful of wanted posters were nailed to the wall, fluttering slightly in the breeze.

Nash's gaze caught on one of the posters, a rough sketch of a man with sharp features and dark eyes, the ink faded but unmistakable. He squinted, his gut twisting. It looked a whole lot like Cain. The reward offered wasn't small, either—certainly enough to turn a few heads, especially in a town as rough as this. He knew then with certainty that what the men had said in the store was true.

Nash shifted in his saddle, stealing a glance at Cain, who rode on without so much as a backward look, his expression relaxed, almost carefree. Either he hadn't noticed the poster or he just didn't care. But Nash couldn't shake the uneasy feeling settling over him, the silent confirmation that Cain was carrying more than a few secrets on his back.

Cain must have sensed Nash's gaze because he looked over, raising an eyebrow with a faint smirk. "Somethin' catch your eye back there?"

Nash hesitated, debating whether to say anything. He could feel the weight of his own doubt pressing down, but there was something about Cain's easy grin, the lightness in his tone, that made him hold his tongue.

"Just an old memory," Nash replied, his voice neutral as he nudged his horse forward. "Place like this has a way of stirrin' 'em up."

Cain chuckled, giving a nod of understanding. "Ain't that the truth." He glanced back toward the town, his gaze lingering for a moment. "A place like that has its own shadows, but they're easy enough to leave behind."

Nash grunted, turning his attention back to the trail. He didn't press further, but the image of that wanted poster lingered in his mind, the name and details burned into his memory. Whatever Cain's past was, it was bound to catch up with him eventually—and Nash wasn't sure if he'd be able to keep looking the other way when it did.

Nash and Cain rode out of town, the tension between them thick as dust. Nash kept his eyes on the trail ahead, his jaw clenched, replaying the last exchange with Cain in his mind. Cain, however, rode with an easy calm, his shoulders relaxed, and his hat pulled low against the sun. After a few minutes of silence, Cain gave a low chuckle, breaking the stillness between them.

"What's so funny?" Nash asked, his tone edged with irritation.

Cain smirked, casting a quick glance over at him. "Ah, just thinkin' about that saloon owner back there. His name's Gerry. Owes me a tidy sum of money and has for a while now. Used to make himself scarce whenever he saw me comin'. Today was the first time he didn't have much of a choice."

Nash raised an eyebrow, his curiosity getting the better of him. "And? You finally got him to pay up?"

"Oh, you better believe it," Cain replied, his grin widening. "Cornered him right there behind the bar. Tried givin' me some sob story about slow business and hard times, but I wasn't havin' any of it. Told him I'd let his debts go if he handed over two things: the cash and the best bottle of whiskey in the place."

"And he just handed it over?" Nash asked.

Cain laughed, nodding. "Well, let's just say my charm's hard to resist. That and a little bit of 'persuasion.'" He gave Nash a wink, clearly pleased with himself. "Got every last coin he owed, plus this." Cain patted his saddlebag, where a bottle of dark amber whiskey peeked out.

"So you're tellin' me we got some whiskey waitin' for us tonight?" Nash asked.

Cain nodded, that mischievous glint back in his eye. "Figured it'd make for a good peace offering. And if you're lucky, I might even let you have the first sip."

Nash shook his head, a reluctant smile breaking through. "Guess you're not all trouble, Cain. Just most of it."

They rode on in silence, and as the sun began to set, they found a good spot to make camp, hidden in a small grove with just enough cover from the main trail. They settled in, and after a simple meal, Cain pulled out the bottle, his grin widening as he held it up to the firelight.

"Here's to old debts paid and new ones forgotten," Cain said, handing Nash the bottle.

Nash took it, studying Cain's face in the firelight. The man was a mystery, no doubt about it, but in that moment, with the warmth of the whiskey spreading through him and the easy laughter between them, he found himself letting down his guard. He took a long swig and handed the bottle back, feeling the tension melt away.

As the bottle made its way back to Cain's hands, he took a long pull, the firelight dancing over his face, casting shadows that made his expression hard to read. He let out a sigh, almost as if resigning himself to something, and then glanced over at Nash, his gaze sharper and more intent than it had been all evening.

"I saw it too, you know," Cain said, his voice low and roughened by the whiskey. He shifted, holding the bottle loosely, his thumb running over the glass. "That wanted poster back in town."

Nash stiffened slightly but said nothing, waiting for Cain to go on.

"Figure it's only fair you know the story," Cain continued, his gaze dropping to the fire. "Happened a while back, in a little town farther west. I'd been runnin' with a couple of other fellas back then. They weren't much—just drifters like me, but we had some good times. One night, though..." Cain shook his head, a rueful smile tugging at the corners of his mouth. "One night, the three of us got it in our heads to take on the bank. It wasn't exactly a well-thought-out plan. Hell, it wasn't thought out at all."

He chuckled, a dry, humorless sound, and took another sip. "Those two fools were drunk as skunks, talkin' big about how easy it'd be, how much money we'd make. I wasn't too keen on it, truth be told, but I went along anyway. Figured I'd just keep 'em from gettin' themselves killed. But when we walked in there, guns drawn, the damn security guard was already ready. Guess someone had tipped him off—or maybe he just wasn't as asleep as we thought he'd be."

Cain paused, staring into the fire, the memories flickering in his eyes as clearly as the flames. "Next thing I know, shots are flyin'. Those two fools charged in, guns blazin', and within seconds, both of 'em were down. Dead as stones before they even knew what hit 'em."

Nash watched him closely, sensing the weight of something deeper in Cain's words.

"Only thing I could do was run," Cain muttered, his voice softening. "Got the hell out of there, rode till my horse was nearly dead, and didn't look back. Since then, every now and again, I see my face up on one of those posters. Remindin' me of a mess I didn't start but sure as hell got caught up in."

He returned the bottle to Nash, his expression a mix of regret and resignation. "So, that's the story, Nash. A fool's errand with a couple of drunkards that turned me into a wanted man."

Nash took the bottle, nodding slowly as he absorbed Cain's story. He could hear the rough truth in Cain's voice, the weary acceptance of a man who'd made his choices but wasn't proud of them. And as they sat there, passing the bottle in silence, Nash felt his doubts ease just a little more, the warmth of trust settling back in, one sip at a time.

Cain chuckled, though the sound was humorless. "Trouble's a stubborn creature, Nash. Once it sets its sights on you, it don't let go easy. But I ain't here to drag you down with me. If I thought you couldn't handle it for a second, I'd be long gone."

CHAPTER SEVEN

The afternoon sun hung high, casting long shadows over the narrow trail as Nash and Cain rode side by side in companionable silence. The path twisted through the rugged desert, framed by rocky outcrops that seemed to rise like ancient guardians against the endless sky. Nash's mind lingered on the wanted poster he'd glimpsed back in town, the image still fresh—a constant reminder of the risk he was taking by riding with a marked man.

Ahead, a lone figure appeared on the trail, still as a statue atop his horse, a dark silhouette against the dust-blown horizon. Nash's instincts prickled immediately, his hand hovering near his revolver.

"Looks like we got company," he muttered under his breath.

Cain's gaze narrowed, his eyes flashing with a wary alertness, but he kept his expression carefully neutral. As they closed the distance, the figure straightened in his saddle, his eyes zeroing in on Cain with a look of cold, focused satisfaction. Nash took in the details—rangy frame, rough beard, rifle slung across his back. This was a man who'd come prepared for a fight.

"Well, well," the man drawled, his voice low and gravelly. "Look who I found wanderin' out here. Been lookin' for you, Cain."

Cain's face hardened, his jaw tightening. "Don't know you, stranger," he replied coldly, his hand easing toward his gun.

"Oh, but I know you," the bounty hunter said, pushing his hat back to reveal a pair of sharp, unblinking eyes. "Cain, isn't it? There's a price on your head, and today's the day I'm collectin'."

Cain's fingers brushed the handle of his revolver, his voice dropping into a dangerous tone. "You might want to think twice about that. Ain't worth what you're gonna lose."

The bounty hunter chuckled, but it was a humorless sound. "I think I'll take my chances." He shifted, his hand drifting toward his rifle, the barrel already leveled in their direction. "Step aside, stranger," he said to Nash, his tone dismissive. "This here's between me and Cain."

But Nash's grip tightened on his Colt, his own gun coming up to match Cain's in a heartbeat. He steadied his aim, his voice calm but laced with steel. "That so? Funny because I'd say you made it my business the second you started drawin' down on my partner here."

The bounty hunter's eyes flicked between them, calculating. His rifle gave him the range, but against two drawn revolvers, the odds had shifted out of his favor. He glared at Cain, the threat still heavy in his gaze, but his hand relaxed slightly, lowering the rifle.

"You boys think you're clever," he muttered, his eyes hardening. "But this don't end here, Cain. I'll find you again. And when I do, it'll be the last time."

Cain's expression didn't change, but a faint, cold smile curved his lips. "You do that," he said softly. "But next time, bring more than just yourself if you plan on collecting."

The bounty hunter held Cain's gaze a moment longer, the hostility thick between them, before he jerked his reins, turning his horse sharply. With a last glance back, he rode off, his silhouette shrinking against the afternoon light, a promise of trouble on the horizon.

As he disappeared, Cain holstered his gun with a casual flick, that faint smile still lingering on his face. Nash studied him, his own Colt still in hand.

"You didn't have to bait him like that," Nash said, his tone controlled but edged with frustration. "Could've walked away without a fight."

Cain shrugged, adjusting his hat with an easy calm. "A man like that? He'd have hunted me down no matter what I said. Better he knows what he's dealing with."

Nash exhaled, a mix of relief and wariness lingering. "You didn't even flinch."

Cain's eyes met his, hard and unapologetic. "When you've been on the run as long as I have, you learn not to flinch."

As the dust settled behind the departing bounty hunter, Cain glanced over at Nash, his expression unreadable momentarily. Then, a slow, almost amused smile tugged at the corner of his mouth. "Well," he drawled, adjusting his hat, "didn't expect you to stand by me like that, Nash. Figured you'd let the bounty hunter have his money."

Nash shrugged, holstering his Colt. "I don't much care for folks who go lookin' to pick a fight."

Cain chuckled, a sound warmer than his usual guarded tone. "That may be, but most folks would've taken a step back and let me handle it. You..." He paused, searching Nash's face as if seeing him in a new light. "You didn't even hesitate."

Nash looked away, feeling the weight of Cain's gaze. "I'm a man who's been in his fair share of tight spots. Sometimes, you don't get to pick who's at your side when things get rough. Figured we're ridin' together, so I wasn't about to leave you to handle it alone."

Cain nodded a rare openness in his expression. "That's more than most would do. You know... I'm not used to folks backin' me up like that. Been a long time since anyone did."

Nash studied him, noting the subtle flicker of vulnerability beneath Cain's usually impenetrable exterior. For once, Cain's face was free of that hard, calculating edge, replaced with something that looked almost... grateful.

Cain broke the silence with a quiet laugh. "Guess I oughta thank you, though. You didn't have to do it."

Nash gave a slight nod, feeling a strange satisfaction at the gratitude in Cain's voice.

Cain's grin widened, and he gave Nash a respectful nod. "Reckon I'm glad it's you I got ridin' with me, Nash."

They continued on, a new layer of understanding between them. For all his secrets and shadows, Cain's reaction made Nash feel that maybe, just maybe, he'd made the right choice in not walking away when the Comanche had set upon Cain.

They made camp under a blanket of stars, the fire crackling softly, casting a warm glow over the rocky terrain. As Nash set up his bedroll, Cain rummaged through his saddlebag and pulled out a second bottle of whiskey, holding it up with a mischievous glint in his eye.

"Didn't know you had another one stashed," Nash said, a grin tugging at his mouth as he reached for it.

Cain held it just out of reach, a smirk playing on his face. "Ah, not so fast, Nash. You want a drink, you're gonna have to earn it."

Nash raised an eyebrow. "Earn it, huh? And what exactly do I need to do?"

Cain stretched out on the ground, resting his head on his saddle as he twisted the bottle open and took a slow sip, clearly savoring it. "Simple," he said, leaning back with a lazy grin. "I want to see you practice your draw. Figure with the day we've had, it wouldn't hurt to keep those skills sharp."

Nash huffed a laugh, shaking his head but unable to hide the amusement in his eyes. "You're really gonna make me work for it, huh?"

"Think of it as motivation," Cain replied, tipping the bottle in a mock toast. "Now, show me what you got."

Nash rolled his shoulders, loosening himself up, and took his stance a few feet from the firelight. He focused, hand hovering near his Colt, letting his mind clear as he drew in a breath.

"Relax," Cain called, his tone easy but with an edge of authority. "You're still too stiff. That's your first mistake—don't think so much. Just let your hand move."

Nash adjusted his stance, feeling the tension ease from his shoulders as he followed Cain's advice. He let his hand move naturally, reaching for the Colt in one smooth motion, drawing it in a practiced arc. The weight felt solid and steady in his grip, and he took aim, holding it firm.

"Better," Cain said, nodding approvingly as he took another sip. "But try not to tense your wrist on the draw. Keep it loose—makes it easier to aim."

Nash nodded, adjusting his grip and trying again, the motion smoother this time. Cain reclined against the saddle, watching him with a critical eye, every so often throwing out bits of advice.

"Good, good. Faster, though," Cain murmured. "You want to be able to clear that holster without hesitatin'. If you're too slow, you might as well hand over your gun."

They continued like this, Cain lounging back, occasionally lifting the bottle to his lips, his voice calm and steady as he guided Nash through each practice draw. With each attempt, Nash felt the movements become more natural, his speed picking up, his aim settling without thought.

Finally, Cain let out a low chuckle, pressing the cork back into the bottle. "All right, Nash, reckon you've earned yourself a drink." He tossed the bottle over, watching with a grin as Nash caught it mid-air.

Nash took a swig, savoring the warmth as it slid down his throat. A rare satisfaction settled over him.

"Not bad," Cain said, nodding in approval. "You keep at it, and you'll be faster than half the folks I've seen draw."

Nash gave a slight nod, tipping the bottle in a small toast. "Well, I'll be sure to keep practicin'. Reckon it'll come in handy, ridin' with you."

Cain chuckled, his eyes glinting in the firelight. "Maybe it will. But one thing's for sure—you got grit, Nash. And that'll keep you alive longer than any gun skill."

The campfire crackled low, casting faint, dancing shadows over the rugged landscape. Nash sat just outside the glow of the firelight, leaning against his saddle with his arms crossed, his gaze fixed on the distant horizon. Cain, on the other side of the flames, lay stretched out with his hat tipped down over his face, silent but awake. A stillness hung between them, broken only by the occasional pop of burning wood.

Cain shifted, tilting his hat back and looking straight into the fire. His eyes seemed darker than usual, the weight of something unspoken hanging heavy in them. For a moment, he looked less like the hardened outlaw Nash had seen at every turn and more like a man who'd seen too much, lost too much.

"You ever had family, Nash?" Cain asked, his voice low and rough, barely louder than a whisper.

The question took Nash by surprise, and he hesitated. "Used to," he replied cautiously, watching Cain closely.

Cain nodded slowly as if that answer confirmed something he'd been thinking. "Me too," he muttered, his gaze distant. "Used to have a lot of things, truth be told. But family... that's the one I've missed the most."

Nash shifted, caught off guard by the uncharacteristic vulnerability in Cain's tone. "What happened to them?"

Cain's face twisted, a bitter smile tugging at the corners of his mouth. "A lot happened, I guess. They were good folks, the kind that don't survive long in a place like this. They tried to keep me out of trouble, tried to make something better of me." His gaze dropped, a shadow passing over his face. "But trouble's like a bad smell. Once you got it on you, it sticks. And sooner or later, it sticks to everyone around you too."

Nash listened in silence, sensing the pain in Cain's words. He knew what it was to lose family, to watch the world take from you until you had nothing left to give. But he hadn't expected to hear it from Cain.

"They're gone now," Cain continued, his voice barely a whisper. "Lost my father first. Bandits took him out over a few dollars and a horse. Then my mother—she couldn't handle it on her own." He stopped, drawing a deep breath, as though the memory of it still clawed at him. "And my younger brother... he was about the only one I had left. Good kid, had a fire in him." Cain's eyes flickered with something raw, and he looked away. "Got himself killed tryin' to defend me. Didn't stand a chance."

Nash felt a heaviness settle over him as he watched Cain, his suspicions tempered by a hint of understanding. Cain was a man marked by tragedy, his ruthlessness a byproduct of survival. A man like that who'd lost everything wouldn't think twice about doing what it took to stay alive.

"They made you pay for it," Nash said quietly, his tone not entirely unsympathetic.

Cain gave a short, humorless laugh. "Yeah. Life's made me pay every day since." He looked up, meeting Nash's gaze, his eyes flickering with a hardness that seemed both defiant and resigned. "I don't expect you to understand, Nash. You seem like the type who's got a code, a way of seeing the world. But me... I stopped believing in rules a long time ago. The only code I got left is to keep breathing and to hell with what anyone else thinks about it."

Nash absorbed Cain's words, his mind racing with conflicting thoughts. He'd heard his fair share of sob stories, from drifters and outlaws alike, men who used their past to justify any crime, any cruelty. But this felt different. Cain wasn't excusing himself; he was simply laying it out, the raw truth of a man who'd had his heart torn out one piece at a time.

"You think that's the only way to live?" Nash asked, his voice calm, though it had an edge of challenge. "Just you against the world, taking what you can, leaving the rest?"

Cain's eyes narrowed a flicker of defiance in them. "Maybe it ain't much of a life. But it's kept me alive this long. Can you say the same?"

Nash held his gaze, feeling the tension coil tighter. "I got my own ways," he said, his tone low but steady. "And I don't drag folks down with me when I go. It's hard enough just tryin' to stay right with yourself."

Cain's mouth twisted into a smirk. "Right with yourself, huh? Ain't no right or wrong in this world, Nash. Just people with guns and people without 'em. The ones with guns win; the ones without, they end up like my brother. Like my folks. You can call it what you want, but that's the truth."

The words hung heavy between them, neither man willing to back down. Nash felt the weight of Cain's past pressing against his own, a bleak reminder of how easily a man could lose himself in the darkness. But he also felt a spark of something else—a challenge, a line he wasn't ready to cross.

"You could make it different," Nash said quietly, almost to himself. "We all got a choice, Cain, even if it's buried under a heap of trouble."

Cain chuckled, shaking his head. "You keep tellin' yourself that, Nash. But I've seen enough of this world to know that some of us don't get choices. We just get the scraps left over when everyone else has taken their fill."

Nash had no reply to that. Instead, he leaned back against his saddle, letting the silence settle around them again. He still didn't trust Cain, didn't know if he ever could. But he'd seen enough of the man's broken edges to understand a little more of what drove him.

As the fire died down, Nash turned his gaze back to the stars, the vast, unchanging sky offering a quiet reminder that there were things bigger than both of them. And as he drifted into a fitful sleep, he couldn't shake the feeling that he was riding alongside a man whose fate was as tangled as his own—one who might be a friend or a foe, but either way, was a danger Nash couldn't ignore.

CHAPTER EIGHT

Hogdson had the look of a place that had seen better days, its glory long faded and settled under a thick layer of dust. The main street stretched in a crooked line, flanked by squat, weather-beaten buildings that seemed to huddle together against the relentless prairie winds. Most had sagging roofs and chipped paint, remnants of once-bright colors now reduced to dull shades of brown and gray, their wooden beams worn smooth from years of sun and sand. A few rickety signs swung lazily from rusted hooks—the saloon, the blacksmith, a barbershop— each barely legible, their letters peeling and faded.

In front of the general store, a horse trough sat half-empty, its water murky with dust and leaves. A few stray dogs lay sprawled in the scant shade offered by the overhanging roofs, their ribs visible beneath patchy fur. Further down the street, a group of children lingered by a broken fence, their eyes wide and curious as they watched the newcomers, but they stayed close to the safety of a weathered old woman, her eyes sharp beneath the brim of a wide straw hat.

A low hum of activity drifted from the saloon, where a handful of men leaned against the railings, glancing sidelong at Nash and Cain as they passed. Most wore wide-brimmed hats pulled low, hiding faces etched with lines from sun, wind, and a lifetime of rough living. The air was thick with the smell of horses, dry earth, and a faint hint of tobacco smoke wafting from somewhere down the street.

As they rode further into the town, Nash felt the quiet weight of the place settle over him, a town teetering on the edge of being forgotten, clinging to life with stubborn resilience. A few townsfolk cast wary glances their way, but Nash barely noticed; he was finally feeling at ease in Cain's company, the recent days of travel building a strange but undeniable bond.

They came to a stop in front of a modest storefront. The general store's painted sign creaked in the breeze, and Nash began dismounting, thinking of the supplies they'd need for the next leg of their journey. But as he turned, he caught the glint in Cain's eye—a look that was as familiar as it was unsettling.

"Cain," Nash said slowly, his voice tinged with suspicion, "we're just here for supplies, right?"

Cain smirked, his gaze shifting to the store's entrance. "Supplies... of a kind," he replied, patting the handle of his revolver in a way that made Nash's stomach drop.

"What're you talkin' about?" Nash demanded, his voice low but tense.

Cain flashed him a grin, his tone relaxed as he tilted his head toward the door. "Just a quick stop, Nash. Stick with me—you won't regret it."

Nash wanted to argue, to pull Cain back, but the easy confidence in Cain's voice worked like a spell, drawing him in against his better judgment.

The door to the general store creaked as Nash and Cain stepped inside, the dim light filtering through dusty windows casting a dull glow over the cluttered shelves. The air smelled faintly of stale tobacco and kerosene, mingling with the scent of dried goods and leather. Shelves were lined with everything a small town might need—jars of pickled vegetables, tins of coffee, boxes of nails, and sacks of flour stacked in the corner. Behind the counter, an older man with wire-rimmed spectacles looked up from a ledger, his brow furrowing as he took in the newcomers.

"Afternoon, gents. What can I help you with?"

Cain gave the room a slow, assessing sweep, his gaze lingering on the display case holding cartridges and a couple of knives. Then, he looked back at the storekeeper, a slow smile raising the corners of his mouth as he took a step forward, his hand resting lightly on his belt. "I'm thinkin' you can help us with a bit of cash," he said, his voice smooth and deceptively calm.

The storekeeper's face paled, his eyes flicking nervously between the two men. Nash felt his stomach twist as the meaning behind Cain's words settled over him like a dark cloud. He opened his mouth to protest, but Cain had already drawn his gun, aiming it at the storekeeper with the easy, practiced confidence of a man who'd done it a hundred times before.

"Hand it over," Cain continued, his tone steady, almost friendly. "We're just passin' through, but we'd be much obliged if you made it worth our while."

The storekeeper's hands trembled as he backed up a step, his gaze darting to Nash as if seeking some kind of mercy or explanation. Nash's chest tightened, and for a brief moment, he felt the urge to step between them, somehow defusing the situation. But Cain caught his eye, his gaze hard and unyielding, warning him against any interference.

The weight of Cain's stare seemed to force Nash's own hand to his Colt, and before he fully registered what he was doing, he had drawn his gun, leveling it at the terrified man behind the counter. His heart hammered in his chest, the reality of what he was doing sinking in like a stone, but he kept his hand steady.

"What're you doin'?" the storekeeper stammered, his voice barely more than a whisper, his gaze locked on Nash.

Nash swallowed, his throat dry. He held his gun firm, but his voice shook just enough to betray him. "Just... do what he says," he muttered, his own disbelief bleeding through every word. How had he ended up here, holding a gun on an innocent man?

"In there," Cain threw a small empty bag across the counter towards the storekeeper.

The storekeeper hesitated, his hands hovering over the register as if still hoping for some kind of reprieve. But one look at Cain's cold, unyielding expression drove him to action. With shaking hands, he opened the cash drawer, pulling out bills and coins, stacking them into a leather bag with a reluctance that only deepened the sick feeling in Nash's gut.

Cain watched with an expression of detached amusement, leaning casually against the counter as if he were merely a customer waiting for his change. As the storekeeper handed over the bag, Cain plucked it from his grasp with a satisfied grin, tossing it in the air before catching it with a showy flick of his wrist.

"Much appreciated," he said, tipping his hat in a mock gesture of respect. Then, with a glance over his shoulder, he sauntered toward the shelves, his eyes glinting with interest as he took stock of the store's other offerings.

Cain moved with an air of absolute confidence, reaching for two bottles of whiskey and setting them on the counter as if they were simply items on a shopping list. He grabbed a box of cartridges, turning it over in his hand with an approving nod before setting it next to the liqor. Further down the aisle, he paused by the packs of beef jerky, grabbing a handful, all while keeping an eye on the storekeeper with a wry grin.

"Help yourself, Cain," Nash muttered under his breath, unable to hide the bitterness creeping into his voice. But he kept his gun trained on the storekeeper, feeling trapped between the threat of Cain's expectations and his own twisted sense of loyalty.

Cain flashed him a grin, raising one of the whiskey bottles as if in a toast. "Don't mind if I do. After all, a man's gotta make the most of his time." He twisted off the cap, taking a swig before setting it back on the counter with a satisfied sigh.

The storekeeper watched in horrified silence, his eyes wide and pleading. Nash felt the weight of the man's gaze, his heart pounding with the shame of what he'd done. Every instinct screamed at him to end this, to tell Cain enough was enough, but he could feel the trap tightening around him, the realization that he was in too deep.

As Cain finally gathered the last of his spoils, he glanced back at the storekeeper, his tone shifting to a mocking politeness. "Now, be a good fella and don't go runnin' to the sheriff for a while. We're just passin' through, and it'd be a real shame to get folks stirred up over nothin'."

The storekeeper nodded mutely, his face drained of color as he clutched the counter for support. Without another word, Cain gestured for Nash to follow, and they stepped out into the bright afternoon sunlight, the door swinging shut behind them.

The heat of the sun felt almost oppressive as they mounted their horses, Cain kicking his mount into a quick trot without so much as a backward glance. Nash followed, the sick weight of what he'd done settling over him as they rode out of town, leaving a trail of dust in their wake.

They didn't stop until they were miles out, the town a distant speck on the horizon. Cain finally reined in his horse, and a low chuckle escaped his lips, building into a full-throated laugh that echoed across the empty plains.

"Well, Nash," he said, patting the bag of stolen cash with a grin, "looks like you're one of us now. Reckon the law won't look too kindly on you after this. Might be seein' your own face on a wanted poster soon enough."

Nash glared at him, his mouth set in a grim line. "You planned this, didn't you?" he demanded, his voice tight with anger. "Wanted to make sure I couldn't turn on you, that I'd have somethin' to lose."

Cain shrugged, his smile never faltering. "Maybe. But I didn't force you, Nash. You pulled that gun yourself. Ain't no one to blame but you." His voice was smooth, almost casual, but there was an edge in his eyes that sent a chill through Nash.

Nash's jaw clenched, his hands tightening on the reins. He felt a bitter mix of shame and anger, the weight of his own actions pressing down on him. He'd wanted to believe in Cain, to trust that there was more to the man than his shadows, but now he could see the trap for what it was.

Cain reached into his saddlebag, pulling out one of the whiskey bottles he'd taken from the store. He held it out to Nash, his expression softening just slightly. "Might as well drink to it," he said, his tone almost sincere. "Ain't many men would ride with me like you just did."

Nash hesitated, his mind spinning with everything that had just happened, but he took the bottle, lifted it to his lips, and let the burn of the whiskey drown out the bitterness. As he lowered the bottle, he felt a hollow ache settle in his chest, the sharp realization that he was now as marked as Cain, tied to a man who'd just stripped away the last of his innocence.

They rode on in silence. The camaraderie of the past few days soured into something darker, something that felt like chains tightening around his wrists. As the sun dipped low over the hills, Nash knew with a cold certainty that there was no turning back. Cain's stories of his family and his acts of seeming kindness to help Nash improve his draw had all been false. Cain had used them to tie Nash to him.

As Nash rode through the quiet, open landscape, the weight of his realization pressed down on him like a stone in his gut. He thought back on all those nights around the campfire, Cain's easy laughter, the stories he'd shared of his family, the tales that had seemed to hint at some depth beyond the hardened exterior. Cain had painted himself as a man who'd just made a few wrong choices, who carried regrets as deeply as Nash did, a man who'd lost things he couldn't get back.

And yet, here in the fading light of day, Nash could see it all for what it was: an act. Every story, every gesture, even the acts of kindness—Cain had crafted them carefully, drawing Nash closer, tying him tighter to his side with every word. The way he'd helped Nash improve his draw, the nights they'd shared stories and whiskey, the camaraderie he'd offered—all of it had served one purpose: to keep Nash close, to make sure he couldn't, or wouldn't, walk away.

Nash's jaw clenched as he considered the cold truth. Cain had never wanted a friend or a companion. He wanted a gun. Someone he could rely on when things got rough, a buffer between him and the bullets that were bound to come his way. Nash was little more than a shield, a tool Cain could use to protect himself. And the kindness, the friendliness? It had all been bait.

The bitter sting of betrayal settled in Nash's chest as he pieced it all together. Every time he'd faltered, every time he'd questioned Cain's intentions, Cain had countered with a smooth story or a friendly smile, something to keep Nash's doubts at bay. Cain had seen his need for trust, his own search for something better than the lonely trails he'd wandered, and he'd used it to pull Nash in closer.

The realization filled Nash with a slow-burning anger, but there was something deeper, too—a hollow ache, the hurt of a man who'd been strung along by the one person he'd let himself trust. Cain had used him, chipped away at his morals and turned him into something he wasn't, all to make sure he'd never have to ride alone. He'd tied Nash to him with invisible chains, slowly and skillfully, until there was no easy way out.

Cain had made him a part of his dark world, and he couldn't undo that. But as the sun dipped lower, casting long shadows over the landscape, Nash resolved that he wouldn't be used any longer. One way or another, he'd find a way to break free, to untangle himself from the web of lies Cain had spun around him. But for the moment, he was going to have to play along.

CHAPTER NINE

The morning was clear, with a soft sun rising above the rolling plains, casting golden light over the rough landscape as Nash and Cain rode side by side. The quiet was welcome, each man absorbed in his own thoughts, neither saying much. Nash kept a careful eye on Cain, who rode with that unsettling ease of his, as if the world behind them wasn't on fire.

They hadn't ridden far when Nash felt a prickling along the back of his neck, the kind of feeling he'd learned not to ignore. He slowed his horse, casting a glance over his shoulder, his eyes scanning the horizon. At first, there was nothing but open land, the same rugged stretches of rock and grass he'd been seeing for days, but as his gaze swept back a second time, he saw it—a faint dust cloud kicking up in the distance.

Nash's gut tightened. "We've got company," he muttered to Cain, who pulled his horse around to see.

Cain's face went cold. "How many?"

"Looks like three, maybe four."

Cain's eyes narrowed, and for a second, Nash could have sworn he saw something like satisfaction flash across Cain's face. Cain nodded and adjusted his rifle in its holster. "Well, looks like they want a fight."

Nash scowled, scanning the horizon again. "Cain, we don't know what they want—"

A gunshot cracked through the air, the report sharp and unmistakable. A bullet whizzed past, missing them by inches, sending a small plume of dust into the air where it hit the ground nearby. The horses skittered and reared, their hooves pawing the dirt.

"Damn it," Nash muttered, swinging his horse around. He cast a quick glance at Cain, who was already drawing his gun, his expression hard and ruthless.

"Run or fight?" Cain shouted, cocking his rifle with a swift motion.

Nash's instincts screamed to run— they were in open country, and staying in a gunfight against men with the high ground was suicide. But he also knew that if he showed any hesitation, Cain would stand his ground, guns blazing, likely dragging Nash down with him.

"Let's get to those rocks!" Nash pointed to a jagged outcrop a few hundred yards away, offering at least a sliver of cover.

They spurred their horses, galloping hard toward the outcrop as bullets tore through the air around them. Another shot rang out, closer this time, and Nash saw a puff of dirt rise beside him as the shot narrowly missed his leg. He grit his teeth and urged his horse on, adrenaline surging as they reached the rocks and slid down behind cover, their horses whinnying in protest.

Cain wasted no time, swinging his rifle up, resting it on a rock, and returning fire with quick, deadly precision. Nash pulled his own gun, scanning the ridges for any sign of their attackers, and spotted a rider silhouetted against the morning sky. He steadied his aim and squeezed the trigger, watching as the figure jerked in the saddle, his arm flinging up before he toppled sideways out of view.

"Good shot," Cain grunted, cocking his rifle for another round, his expression intent and focused.

For a brief, dangerous moment, they held their ground, shots echoing off the rocks as they traded fire with the vigilantes. Nash could feel his heart pounding, the heat of the sun bearing down on them, his hands slick on the revolver's grip. He glanced over at Cain, who fired each shot with a practiced ruthlessness that sent chills through him. It was clear Cain wasn't just holding his ground; he was enjoying this.

Nash took a moment to reload, his breath ragged as he slid fresh cartridges into the cylinder. He glanced back toward the horizon, catching a glimpse of the remaining riders regrouping, pulling back slightly as they assessed their next move.

"Looks like they're deciding whether it's worth their trouble," Nash muttered.

"Let 'em decide," Cain said coldly, leveling his rifle and firing again, the shot cracking the air like a whip.

But Nash's patience was running thin. He holstered his revolver, looking back toward the open expanse behind them. "We need to ride, Cain. They'll bring reinforcements, and I don't fancy sticking around for a second wave."

Cain reluctantly nodded, pulling his rifle back with one last lingering glance at the retreating riders. They mounted quickly, spurring their horses into a fast gallop away from the rocky outcrop and into the cover of a winding trail that dipped between the hills. They rode hard, and neither man looked back as they put distance between themselves and the gunmen.

It was nearly an hour before they slowed, the rush of the gunfight still lingering in the air between them. Nash pulled his horse to a stop, glancing sidelong at Cain, who seemed unfazed, his expression calm as if he hadn't just been in a shootout.

"Don't fool yourself, Cain," Nash replied, his tone cold. "I don't make a habit of dragging trouble along for the ride. Seems like trouble's got its hooks in you plenty deep."

Cain's eyes narrowed, a dangerous glint flashing in them. "You sure about that, Nash? We've been riding together long enough—trouble's a two-way road."

Nash's grip tightened on his reins, and for a moment, they stared each other down, a silent challenge simmering between them. But he knew better than to push it—Cain was volatile and unpredictable, and Nash wasn't eager to draw his gun on a man he knew was faster than he was. Even so, the seeds of doubt had taken root, and Nash couldn't shake the feeling that Cain was hiding more than just a violent past and worse, Nash was now becoming a part of Cain's story.

Without another word, he turned his horse, leading the way down the trail, his thoughts tangled and heavy. Every instinct told him to cut Cain loose, to ride out on his own and leave this trouble behind. But something kept him bound to the man, some thread of curiosity—or maybe a need for justice—that he couldn't ignore.

As they rode on, the silence grew thick and tense, each man lost in his own thoughts. Nash kept a wary eye on Cain, his hand never straying far from his holster. One way or another, he knew this partnership was nearing its end—and when it did, he intended to be the one standing when the dust settled.

They'd set up camp under a clear sky, the fire crackling softly between them as the stars began to flicker above. Nash sat in silence, stirring the embers with a stick, his mind restless and uneasy. He'd been turning things over in his head, the realization of Cain's manipulation weighing on him. But before he could retreat too deeply into his thoughts, Cain broke the quiet with a low chuckle.

"You know," Cain drawled, leaning back against his saddle with a grin, "from the moment I laid eyes on you, I knew I was gonna keep you at my side. Figured you'd be the perfect fit."

Nash glanced up, his eyes narrowing. "That so?"

"Oh, sure," Cain continued, unfazed by the chill in Nash's tone. "Took me about five seconds to figure out you've got some Indian blood in you. Can always tell. And I knew I'd be a damn fool to let you out of my sight."

Cain's grin widened as he gestured at Nash with the whiskey bottle. "Folks like you, you've got that sixth sense. Like today—you sensed those gunmen behind us before they even showed themselves. That's somethin' no white man I've known could ever do. Figured it was high time I made sure to keep you close."

Nash's jaw clenched, a flare of anger surging through him. It was the first time Cain had mentioned anything about his heritage, and the casual way he threw it out as if it was some kind of tool, some piece of his identity to be exploited—it grated on Nash's last nerve.

"So that's it, huh?" Nash replied, his voice low, laced with a cold edge. "You've kept me around like some kind of hunting dog, a lucky charm, 'cause you think I got some mystical sense you can use?"

Cain shrugged, his grin unfaltering. "Don't take it so hard, Nash. I'm just speakin' plain. Never met an Indian who didn't have a way with things, some kind of gift for stayin' alive and knowin' what's out there."

Nash's hands tightened into fists, his gaze hard as he stared across the fire at Cain. "You think you got me all figured out, don't you?" he said, barely containing his anger. "Just 'cause I got some blood that's different from yours, you reckon I'm somethin' other than a man. Just somethin' to keep you out of trouble."

Cain rolled his eyes, taking another swig from the bottle. "Oh, come on now, Nash. Ain't no need to get all worked up over it. It's just facts, as far as I see it. You got that blood in you, gives you an edge most men don't have. Ain't my fault if that works in my favor."

Nash forced himself to breathe slowly, letting the firelight dance over his clenched fists as he tried to keep his voice steady. "You talk about me like I'm some kind of tool, Cain. Somethin' to use when it's convenient, just like every other damn thing you take."

Cain's smile faltered slightly, but he quickly recovered, shrugging again. "Guess I just see things practical-like, Nash. You're free to go anytime you want. But you keep stickin' around, so I reckon we're both gettin' somethin' out of this, ain't we?"

Nash shook his head, feeling a bitter resolve settle within him. Cain's words had laid things bare—he was nothing more than a means to an end in Cain's eyes. Looking across the fire, he realized he couldn't let himself be manipulated; his heritage was twisted into something useful only when it served Cain's purposes.

For the rest of the night, Nash said nothing more. He sat by the fire, watching the embers slowly burn down, his mind clear with a new determination. Whatever reason Cain thought he had to keep him close, Nash knew he was done playing along. And soon, he'd be ready to make his own choice, one Cain wouldn't see coming.

CHAPTER TEN

The dawn had barely crept over the hills when the first shot rang out, slicing through the crisp morning air. Nash snapped awake, instincts taking hold as he grabbed his Colt and rolled to the side, feeling a bullet whiz by his head. A split-second later, Cain scrambled up beside him, already returning fire in short, sharp bursts.

"Over there!" Nash shouted, his eyes scanning the shadows for more movement. He counted at least half a dozen figures, crouched low and moving in on them. Shots echoed, the smell of gunpowder thickening in the air. "There's at least six."

Cain's face was a mask of fury, his grip sure as he fired ruthlessly. "This your idea of a quiet morning?" he shouted to Nash over the noise, his tone edged with grim humor. But Nash wasn't laughing.

Another round tore through the rocks beside him, spraying him with shards of stone. "We're sittin' ducks here," Nash yelled back, barely able to hear himself. "We need cover!"

He gestured toward a ridge about a hundred yards off, and Cain nodded, his gaze calculating as he assessed their odds. They'd have to run for it.

"On three," Nash called, breathing hard. "One... two... three!"

They burst from the cover of their camp, kicking up dust as they sprinted toward the ridge. Shots cracked behind them, bullets chewing up the ground around their feet. Nash's heart pounded with each step, adrenaline pushing him forward. As they reached the slope, he threw himself behind a boulder, feeling his pulse race as Cain landed beside him.

A few tense moments passed, and then everything went silent. Nash stole a glance over the ridge, seeing the gunmen regrouping, their eyes scanning the hillside.

"Is that price on your head worth dyin' for," Nash muttered, reloading his revolver. He caught Cain's gaze, and for a brief moment, Cain's hardened expression softened, a flicker of unease showing through.

"These men—they're not after you, Nash," Cain replied, his voice tight. "It's me they want. I'll draw 'em off if it comes to it."

Nash bristled, his instinct to survive battling with a strange sense of loyalty, even though he was fairly sure Cain was only making the offer to ensure Nash stayed at his side. He knew Cain now well enough. He also knew that in the face of six gunmen they were better off together.

In the middle of the gunfight, a sharp pain seared through Nash's shoulder as a bullet grazed him, sending a shock up his arm. The wound wasn't deep, but he could feel the strength starting to drain from his arm, his aim growing less steady. He gritted his teeth, ducking back behind a boulder, blood staining the sleeve of his shirt.

Cain caught sight of the blood, his face darkening with frustration. "Hell, Nash, can't you go five minutes without takin' a hit?" he snapped, eyes narrowing with barely concealed irritation.

Nash shot him a glare. "Maybe they ought to have you instead," he retorted. "You're a damn magnet for trouble, Cain, and sooner or later, it's gonna get us both killed."

Cain's eyes flashed with anger. "I never asked you to stick around, Nash. You got a choice."

The only sounds around them were the crack of gunfire and the settling dust.

"Damn it," Nash muttered under his breath, shaking his head. "Let's just finish this."

With a curt nod, they turned back to face the gunmen, their weapons ready.

Nash's arm throbbed, but he forced himself to ignore it, his Colt aimed and steady. The men had drawn closer, their eyes fixed on them with grim determination, guns raised ready to fire.

Nash moved first, squeezing off a shot, the crack of his Colt echoing across the rocky terrain. Cain's rifle roared beside him, each shot precise, deadly, and as controlled as if he were practicing. Together, they moved from cover to cover, ducking behind rocks, their shots ringing out in unison, their timing and precision a deadly rhythm that left the gunmen with no choice but to fall back.

One by one, the attackers went down or scrambled to retreat, the last two scattering into the distance. When the dust settled, the only sound left was the quiet crackle of rocks dislodging from their cover. Nash exhaled, his grip loosening on the Colt as he lowered it, the ache in his shoulder finally sinking in.

He holstered his gun, glancing over at Cain, who was watching him with an unreadable expression, dust and sweat streaking his face. There was something in his eyes—something fierce, almost desperate—but Nash wasn't sure if it was anger or something else. What he did know was that Cain was more than just a man on the run. He was a lightning rod for danger, a live wire with enemies on every side, and somehow, Nash had gotten himself caught in the crossfire.

Cain met his gaze, a strange intensity lingering in his eyes. "Still thinkin' about takin' off, Nash?"

Nash didn't answer, just tightened his jaw and looked away, feeling the weight of everything that had happened, every scrape and wound he'd taken in Cain's company. As they set off again, the silence between them was heavy, the tension thicker than the dust clinging to their boots.

The desert night settled over them like a heavy blanket, the air cool and quiet after the day's blistering heat. Nash sat near the fire, binding his wounded shoulder with a torn strip of his shirt, wincing as he tightened the makeshift bandage. The embers crackled softly, casting flickering shadows across the ground, and for a moment, he allowed himself to settle into a rare silence. But across the fire, Cain's eyes were fixed on him, unreadable and darker than the night.

Nash noticed the change in him immediately. Cain hadn't said much since the gunfight earlier, his usual smirk absent, replaced with a calculating, distant look. There was no trace of camaraderie, none of the teasing or casual indifference Nash had grown used to. Instead, Cain's gaze was cold, assessing, as if he were weighing Nash's worth.

When Nash finally spoke, his voice was strained. "That was close today. Could've gone worse if I hadn't seen those gunmen first."

Cain's expression didn't change. He glanced over at Nash, taking in the bandage and the bloodstained shirt, before letting out a low, humorless chuckle. "Trouble's what keeps men like us alive," he said, his tone colder than the desert air. "But I can't afford dead weight, Nash. And that wound of yours... it'll slow you down."

Nash froze, and he looked up, studying Cain's face with a new suspicion. "What're you gettin' at?"

Cain sighed, an exaggerated gesture, as if disappointed. "I can't be patchin' you up every few miles."

Before Nash could respond, he saw the shift in Cain's eyes, a quick, predatory gleam. Cain's hand moved to his belt, the glint of his revolver catching in the firelight. In one fluid motion, he raised it, pointing it squarely at Nash.

"Hand over your money," Cain said, his voice a chilling calm. "And your guns."

Nash's heart pounded as the betrayal sank in. He looked into Cain's eyes, searching for some trace of the man he thought he'd known, but there was nothing there but cold resolve. "Cain," he said slowly, his voice low, laced with restrained fury, "what the hell do you think you're doin'?"

Cain's mouth twisted into a faint smirk, but there was no humor in his gaze. "Survivin', Nash. You're a liability. Always askin' questions, second-guessin' me. I don't need anyone draggin' me down—or lookin' over my shoulder and now you're bleeding you're just dead weight. Now, make it easy on yourself and hand over your gun."

Nash's jaw tightened as he took in the situation, his mind racing. Cain was close, the gun aimed directly at his chest, finger resting on the trigger. He was a heartbeat away from squeezing it, and Nash knew any wrong move could turn lethal.

"You really gonna shoot me?" Nash challenged, his voice steady but his words carrying an edge of disbelief. "After all we've been through?"

Cain didn't flinch, his gaze cold and unyielding. "This ain't about friendship, Nash. You're useful until you're not, and right now... you're a risk I can't take."

A bitter laugh escaped Nash as he absorbed the depth of Cain's betrayal. He'd been fooled, drawn in by Cain's stories, his charm, all for this. But as the anger simmered beneath his calm exterior, he slowly raised his hands.

"All right, Cain," he said evenly, his voice betraying none of the fury burning within him. "Take what you want."

Cain stepped closer, keeping his gun trained on Nash as he reached toward the saddlebag, his gaze flickering for just a moment as he focused on the bag's contents.

Seeing his chance, Nash made a swift move, reaching for his belt knife with his good hand. But Cain was quicker. The gun's barrel snapped back up, the cold, metallic click of the hammer cocking.

Nash froze, his hand gripping the knife, knowing he wouldn't be fast enough. Cain's finger flexed on the trigger, his gaze narrowing.

"Nice try," Cain muttered, his voice tinged with irritation. Then, without hesitation, he pulled the trigger.

The shot rang out in the still night, and a searing pain tore through Nash's already wounded shoulder, dropping him to his knees. He gritted his teeth, fighting the surge of agony as he clutched his shoulder, the blood seeping between his fingers. He looked up to see Cain standing over him, his expression void of remorse.

"I told you, Nash. No room for loyalty out here. It's only about what keeps you alive." Cain reached down, yanking Nash's gun from its holster, his grip firm as he tucked it into his belt. "Guess you won't be needin' this."

As Nash sank to the ground, his vision blurring, he felt the weight of his own foolishness. He'd trusted Cain and had thought there was more to him than the outlaw's hardened exterior. But Cain's betrayal was absolute, a final, ruthless severing of any bond they'd shared.

Cain turned and walked back to his horse, mounting with an ease that twisted Nash's stomach. Before he rode off, he cast one last look over his shoulder, his expression hard. "See you around, Nash. Try not to bleed out too quick." With a final, mocking salute, he spurred his horse forward, vanishing into the darkness.

The night closed in, leaving Nash alone in the dust and silence, his own blood pooling beneath him. He clenched his jaw against the pain, his mind ablaze with anger, humiliation, and a fierce, unrelenting resolve. He'd been a fool to trust Cain, but he knew now that he wouldn't let the betrayal go unanswered.

Forcing himself upright, one thought burned in his mind, clear and sharp as the stars overhead. He would find Cain. And when he did, Cain would learn exactly what it meant to betray him. He could never remember how he managed to mount his horse, but he did. He was never sure why Cain had left the mare, the only reason he could think of was that leading a second horse would have slowed him down. Whatever the reason, Nash was grateful; without her, he knew he would have died out on the plains.

CHAPTER ELEVEN

Nash woke to the blinding light of early morning, slicing through thin curtains, stabbing his eyes and sending a dull throb through his head. For a second, he forgot where he was, his mind fogged by exhaustion and pain until he caught sight of his bloodstained shirt hanging over a rickety chair. His shoulder burned, wrapped tightly with bandages, and he let out a slow, pained breath, the memory of Cain's betrayal rushing back with sharp clarity.

"Damn fool," he muttered to himself, shifting to sit up. He winced, the bandaged wound pulling taut, but he forced himself to push through the ache. Somewhere along the line, he'd made his way to this town, a small, quiet place with buildings huddled close together and dust swirling around the worn signs hanging over empty storefronts. He couldn't remember how he'd managed to get here, just that he'd stumbled into town the night before, his strength nearly gone, and had collapsed into this rented bed. Nash, thankfully, hadn't kept all his dollars in the saddle bag, and he'd had enough left to see him right.

A knock at the door startled him, followed by the creak of it opening. A woman in a worn apron stepped in, carrying a water basin and a towel draped over her arm. She gave Nash a quick, assessing glance, noting his injury with a faint look of concern.

"Morning," she said, setting the basin on the small table by the bed. "Looks like you had a rough time of it. Doc Harlon is on his way."

Nash nodded, reaching for the cool towel and pressing it against his face. The woman didn't ask for details, just watched him with a cautious kindness that was hard to come by in places like this.

"I'll fetch you some food," she said, heading toward the door. "If you need anything else, just holler."

Nash thanked her, his voice a raspy murmur, and watched her leave before turning his gaze out the window. The quiet street below stretched into the heart of town. As he sat there, absorbing the silence, he caught sight of the general store across the street. The faded sign hung slightly askew, and a few old barrels sat before it, marking it as a place that'd seen better days.

Nash lay back on the creaky bed, feeling the ache in his shoulder gradually fade as the days passed. The doctor had been by twice already, a gruff older man with a thin gray beard and a tendency to mutter under his breath as he inspected Nash's wound. Each visit brought a new wave of discomfort as the doctor prodded and cleaned the injury, applying a fresh bandage with rough hands.

"Lucky it wasn't worse," the doctor had grumbled during his last visit, peering at Nash with sharp eyes. "Could've gone clean through. You rest up, keep it clean, and you'll be back on your feet soon enough. And don't go thinking you're fit to use that arm for anything heavy just yet."

Nash nodded, his gratitude buried under the discomfort and lingering soreness. "Thanks, Doc."

The doctor had only nodded back, grumbling to himself as he gathered his bag. "Keep to yourself, don't go pickin' at it," he'd said, as if Nash were a troublesome child.

Now, days later, Nash's strength was finally returning, the pain in his shoulder a dull throb rather than the sharp, blinding ache it had been. He managed to sit up in bed for longer stretches, his body slowly adjusting to movement again, and each morning, he found himself stronger, less dependent on the herbs and powders the doctor had left behind.

As the days drifted by in the small boarding house, Nash found himself staring at the ceiling more often than he cared to admit, his thoughts wandering far from the dusty little town and his healing shoulder. He'd lie in bed, the ache in his arm a dull, constant reminder of his choices, but it was nothing compared to the ache somewhere deeper, gnawing at him, a regret that had been creeping in and settling heavy.

Alice.

He could picture her clear as day— her laughter, the way her eyes crinkled at the corners when she smiled, the soft lilt in her voice. In the quiet of the room, his mind would drift back to evenings spent with her, sharing easy conversation, her warmth beside him grounding him in a way nothing else had. She'd always had a way of seeing past his rough edges, calling him out when he tried to keep himself distant, breaking through that armor he wore so well.

And yet, he'd walked away from it all. Left Alice with hardly a word, telling himself he'd return one day, when things were settled, when he'd taken care of the loose ends that seemed to trail him everywhere. He'd wanted to believe he was doing it for the right reasons, that by leaving her behind, he was somehow protecting her from the life he led.

But alone in that quiet room, he couldn't escape the doubt, the nagging thought that maybe he'd been wrong. Perhaps she hadn't needed protecting. Maybe he'd been afraid of letting himself believe in a future with her, one that didn't involve running, hiding, or facing down the barrel of a gun.

He rubbed a hand over his face, his fingers pressing into his eyes as if he could block out the memory of her. He thought of her standing in the doorway, her eyes steady and clear, watching him go. He'd promised himself he'd go back for her, but what kind of promise was that? She deserved more than empty words and fleeting glances over her shoulder.

A sigh escaped him, low and heavy. He hated the feeling of regret—it was foreign and unwelcome, twisting something in his chest whenever he thought of her. The road had always been enough for him, or so he'd thought, but here he was, caught in a rare stillness, realizing that he missed her in a way that made the road feel hollow and endless.

As the sun dipped below the horizon outside his window, casting shadows across the room, Nash felt a sudden, fierce longing to be beside her, to go back and fix his mistakes. He knew he couldn't, not yet. But as he lay back against the pillows, closing his eyes to the dimming light, he made himself a real promise.

When he healed, when he was ready, he'd go back.

Maybe.

One afternoon, as the midday sun filtered through the window, cutting its way between the faded curtains, the woman from the boarding house brought him a bowl of broth and a few slices of bread. She set it down on the side table with a gentle smile.

"You're lookin' better," she remarked, her voice soft but cheerful. "A few more days, and you'll be walkin' around like nothing happened. If you need anythin' else…"

Nash smiling interrupted her, "I know …. just give a holler. Thank you. I appreciate it."

He watched her leave, then turned his gaze towards the window, feeling the quiet weight of the street below. The town lay peaceful, with small clusters of people moving between buildings. The day unfolding slowly as townsfolk went about their business. Across the way, the general store caught his eye, its faded sign creaking slightly in the gentle breeze, a few old barrels stacked out front. The building had a worn look, like most of the town, but something about it pulled at him, a strange sense of familiarity or intuition nudging him.

Maybe it was just the quiet settling over him, but he felt as if the store was holding something he'd missed, something he was meant to find. He'd been focused so long on survival, escape, healing, and moving forward that he hadn't paused to look back.

Finally, after days of waiting, he felt his legs steady beneath him as he rose from the bed. Moving carefully, he shrugged on a clean shirt, leaving the left sleeve loose over his bandaged shoulder. As he took one last look around the room, the weight of his mission settled on him again, clear and certain as ever.

He moved slowly down the stairs, nodding to the woman at the front desk, who gave him an encouraging smile. Stepping out onto the dusty street, he felt the sun's warmth on his skin and took a deep breath. Every step was an effort, his muscles protesting at the strain, but he kept his gaze fixed on the general store, letting the quiet determination pull him forward.

Whatever lay ahead, he knew he was finally ready to face it.

The place smelled of old wood and kerosene, the shelves stocked with the usual assortment of canned goods, ammunition, and tobacco.

Behind the counter stood an older man, grizzled and broad-shouldered, his face marked with scars that hinted at a rough past. He looked up as Nash entered, his eyes narrowing in recognition.

"Well, I'll be," he said, his voice a gravelly drawl. "If it ain't the cowboy Lilly Blackwood's been seeing too. You're not looking too bad. son."

Nash froze, suspicion prickling at his spine. "You got me at a disadvantage, friend."

The man chuckled, the sound rough and gravelly like rocks scraping down a hillside. He stood with his thumbs hooked into his belt, sizing up Nash with a look of equal parts curiosity and amusement. "Name's Dan Holt. You don't know me, but I've heard plenty about you. Lilly found you in the street bleeding all over her steps where you'd fallen from your horse, and she's been looking after you since then. It's a small town; news like that travels mighty fast. So, who put a hole in you, son?"

Nash's gaze drifted past Dan, to the wall behind him, where a cluster of wanted posters was tacked up, each one with a grimy face staring back at him. He lifted a finger, pointing to a poster pinned slightly askew, its edges curling from exposure to the sun. The inked face was unmistakable, a grin frozen on the page, as smug and cold as the real thing.

"He did," Nash replied, his voice tight.

Dan turned, following Nash's finger to the poster, and blew a low whistle. "Cain, huh?" He shook his head, crossing his arms as he took a step closer to the poster, his expression darkening. "Well, son, you've tangled with the meanest rattler in the desert, that's for damn sure. Cain's left a trail of wreckage through these parts. Robbed two banks up north, shot a man down just 'cause he looked at him wrong. Hell, rumor has it he even sold out a whole crew that trusted him, left 'em to rot in some canyon so he could make a clean getaway."

Nash clenched his jaw, feeling the familiar burn of anger simmering in his chest. He'd suspected as much, he'd known Cain was trouble from the start, but hearing the stories laid out so plainly added a new layer of disgust.

Dan continued, ticking off Cain's offenses as though reading from a ledger. "Let's see... a couple of months back, he cleared out a store in Redford and left the owner tied up for two days in the cellar. Took off with all the supplies and didn't even leave a can of beans behind." He gave Nash a long, steady look. "Folks say he's got no loyalty to anyone. You could be his best friend one day and his target the next, all dependin' on what he thinks he can squeeze out of you."

"Sounds about right," Nash muttered, his eyes never leaving the poster.

Dan nodded, the lines in his face deepening. "He's poison, son. One man tried to bring him in a few years back. Cain played nice at first, lured the poor fool in close, and made him feel like he could trust him. Then he turned, shot the man in cold blood, didn't even blink. He's got no conscience. No loyalty, no ties, just a mean streak and a talent for gettin' folks to do his dirty work."

The words hit home, and Nash felt the bitterness coil tighter in his gut. He'd been Cain's pawn, just another fool roped in by the charm, easy smile, and friendly nights around the campfire. All of it had been a setup to keep Nash close until he wasn't useful anymore.

Dan watched him closely, his expression softening slightly. "You're not the first he's crossed, and you sure won't be the last."

Nash gave a grim nod, his eyes hardening. "Well, reckon I owe him one."

Dan's mouth curved into a faint smile. "You're not alone in that. Cain's got more folks gunnin' for him than he can count. And if you ask me…" He glanced at the wanted poster, his expression turning steely. "It's high time someone put him down."

Nash took a long, steadying breath, feeling the weight of his own resolve settle in. "I aim to. First chance I get."

Dan nodded approvingly. "Good to hear. Now, you get yourself patched up, keep your strength. You'll need every ounce if you're goin' after him."

Nash met Dan's gaze, a flicker of gratitude in his eyes. "Thanks. And if you hear anything... anything at all about where he's headed..."

Dan tipped his hat. "You'll be the first to know. Ain't nobody deserves a reckoning more than that cur."

Just before Nash turned to leave, he looked back at the wanted poster, Cain's face staring back at him, that mocking grin frozen in ink. A reckoning was coming, and this time, he'd be ready for it.

Just as Nash reached the door, Dan's voice called out behind him. "Hold up a second, son."

Nash turned, watching as Dan stepped over to the wall. He reached up, fingers brushing over the edges of the worn, sun-bleached wanted poster, Cain's inked face staring out with that infuriating grin. Dan carefully pulled it down, the paper tearing slightly at one corner, and folded it with the precision of someone handling something valuable. He crossed the store towards Nash, the creases in his weathered hands deepening as he pressed the edges of the paper down, making a neat square.

When he reached Nash, he held out the folded poster, his expression solemn.

"Take this," he said, his voice low. "Might not mean much, but it's good to have a reminder of what you're after. Cain's got a way of slippin' through cracks, disappearing like smoke. Keep this close, and don't let yourself forget who he is."

Nash took the poster, feeling the worn paper between his fingers, the edges rough and brittle. The weight of it was surprisingly heavy, a physical reminder of the man he was hunting down, a man who'd nearly cost him his life.

"Thanks," Nash murmured, slipping it inside his vest. The paper crinkled against his side, grounding him in a way he hadn't expected.

Dan gave a single nod, his eyes steady. "Cain's dangerous, son. Meaner than a snake with a broken back."

Nash met Dan's gaze, a shared understanding passing between them. "Reckon, you're right," he said quietly, the steel of determination returning to his voice.

With a final nod, Nash turned, stepping out into the early morning light. The poster weighed against his chest, a silent vow as he mounted his horse and set his sights on the horizon. Cain was out there, somewhere, and Nash knew he wouldn't stop until their paths crossed again.

The days stretched into weeks as Nash lingered in the small, dusty town, his strength returning little by little. Each morning, he'd test his shoulder, rolling it back, feeling the sharp twinge lessen day by day until he could raise his arm without the bite of pain holding him back. The doctor checked in once more, his visits shorter each time, satisfied enough with Nash's recovery to leave him be.

Nash spent his days quietly, watching the townsfolk move about, his focus sharpening with each sunrise. He'd made a promise to himself—a silent, burning vow—that he wouldn't let Cain slip away again, not after what he'd done. And every day spent healing was one more day he'd felt Cain getting farther ahead. The wanted poster Dan had given him stayed tucked in his coat pocket, its worn edges a constant reminder of the man he was after, the face he wouldn't let himself forget.

When he finally felt strong enough, he counted up what was left of his money, sufficient to buy what he'd need and not much more. He'd lost nearly everything he'd had to Cain's betrayal, but he wouldn't leave this town unarmed or unprepared.

Dan, the general store owner didn't say much as Nash stepped inside, only giving him a nod and a polite "Good morning." Nash spent a long moment at the glass counter, his eyes settling on the Colt nestled inside. It was well used, the grip worn with ark nicks in the wood, but Nash knew it would be solid and reliable. When Dan unlocked the cabinet and handed it to him and Nash smiled as he felt the smooth barrel and the grip of a Colt, one his hand recognised. He handed over the bills without hesitation, then added a box of ammunition and a few essential supplies—dried food, a tin cup, and a worn leather water canteen.

Once he'd tucked the items into his saddlebags and loaded the Colt, he stood in the quiet street, taking a deep breath. The town stretched out around him, simple and small, but he felt the weight of his purpose settle over him. He'd rested long enough; it was time to move on.

As he mounted his horse and set off down the dusty road, the town grew smaller behind him, fading into the landscape. The wind picked up, carrying with it the scent of sunbaked earth and open desert, and Nash felt a surge of grim satisfaction. He was ready, armed, and stronger now than when he'd left.

Cain was out there somewhere, and Nash knew he wouldn't stop until he found him. With the weight of the new Colt at his side and the wanted poster tucked against his chest, he felt his purpose sharpen, clearer than ever.

CHAPTER TWELVE

As Nash rode out of town, the world around him seemed sharper, clearer than it had in days. He felt the bite of gravel under his mares hooves, the low hum of cicadas in the brush, and the sun's searing heat as it bore down from an endless blue sky. Each step felt like a stride closer to justice—and revenge. Cain had brought nothing but misery to everyone who crossed his path, and Nash wasn't about to let him leave a trail of blood and lies in his wake.

Nash knew he'd be up against a cunning, ruthless man. Cain didn't just kill; he manipulated and twisted people to get what he wanted. But for the first time since he'd crossed paths with Cain, Nash had an edge—he knew who Cain was, and he had a clear reason to stop him.

The days blurred into one another as he ventured deeper into the wilderness, seeking solitude and the quiet calm of open space. Nash had only the essentials—a canteen, a bedroll, a few supplies—and his new Colt, the polished barrel catching the light every time he reached for it. It was a solid weight at his side, a reminder of the resolve that had been building within him, fueled by the memories of betrayal and the raw ache of his wound.

Mornings were spent under the rising sun, each dawn casting long shadows across the plains as Nash set up small targets, lining up empty bottles and old tin cans in the dust. He'd stand back, gauging the distance, his stance steady and calm. The Colt was unfamiliar at first, the grip slightly different from the one he'd lost, but day by day, he felt it becoming an extension of himself.

He practiced for hours, the sound of gunfire echoing across the empty landscape. His first shots were rusty, his aim thrown by the lingering soreness in his shoulder, but he forced himself to push through it, each pull of the trigger a step closer to strength. He adjusted his stance, rolling his shoulder back to find the angle that wouldn't jar his healing wound, feeling the kick of the gun settle back into a natural rhythm. The targets became easier to hit, each crack of the Colt ringing sharper, more precise.

With every shot, Nash felt his purpose solidify. Cain had been cunning and ruthless, bending people to his will with a mix of charm and cruelty. He didn't just kill—he manipulated and twisted the truth, leaving people broken in his wake.

Nash knew he couldn't afford to be reckless. He'd need a clear mind and a steady hand, and out here, in the isolation of the plains, he found the space to sharpen both.

Evenings brought a stillness to the air, the sun dipping low, painting the horizon in shades of crimson and gold. Nash would set up camp, rolling out his bedroll beneath a star-filled sky. He'd meticulously clean the Colt, dismantling and reassembling it, the metal gleaming in the firelight. Each part felt like a puzzle piece falling into place, steadying his resolve, grounding him in the quiet ritual of preparation.

When the gun was cleaned and his supplies checked, he'd sit by the fire, letting the warmth soak into his skin as he thought of Cain.

Weeks passed the loneliness of the plains transforming from a weight to a kind of solace. His strength returned, his shoulder healed, and his aim grew sharper than it had ever been. With every shot, every practiced movement, he felt himself reclaiming a part of what Cain had tried to take.

Finally, one evening, as he watched the last sliver of sun disappear below the horizon, Nash felt ready. The Colt was familiar in his hand now, the weight of it a promise he intended to keep. He packed his gear carefully, his movements precise, each item placed with purpose.

As dawn broke the following day, Nash mounted his horse and took one last look over the landscape, the plains stretching endlessly before him, filled with both possibility and danger. Cain was out there somewhere, thinking he'd left Nash behind, and had twisted him into something broken.

But he'd underestimated Nash.

With a final, steadying breath, Nash nudged his horse forward, his gaze fixed on the horizon. The pursuit had begun, and he wouldn't stop until Cain faced justice—true justice, this time—and the past he'd tried to outrun was laid to rest for   good.

Nash rode hard for days, the landscape shifting from open plains to jagged hills and rocky terrain as he pushed forward, the purpose that had built within him steadying his hand and sharpening his focus. He'd spent enough time in the quiet solitude of the plains, enough time getting stronger, preparing for this hunt. Now, he was on the move, and each mile felt like a step closer to finding Cain.

The trail led him to Godson, a small town nestled against the edge of a craggy hill range, its cluster of buildings weathered and worn by dust and sun. The town seemed to hold its breath, the streets quieter than most, with only a few townsfolk moving about, their eyes narrowed against the wind, casting Nash curious glances as he rode down the main road.

He pulled up in front of the saloon, a low, crooked building with a sagging porch and paint peeling in long, rough strips from the walls. The faded sign creaked in the breeze, and as Nash dismounted, he felt the weight of curious eyes on him from within.

The saloon was dim and filled with the smell of stale whiskey and sweat. A handful of patrons turned to look at him as he entered, their conversations halting briefly before resuming in low murmurs. Nash approached the bar, pulling the wanted poster from his coat pocket. Its edges were crinkled and worn from days of handling.

The bartender, a thin, wiry man with a patchy beard, glanced up as Nash unfolded the poster and laid it on the counter. Nash tapped the image of Cain with his finger.

"You seen him?" Nash asked, his voice low and calm, though the weight behind his question was unmistakable.

The bartender squinted at the poster, then looked back up at Nash, something cautious in his expression. "Cain, huh?" He scratched his chin, glancing around to ensure no one else was listening too closely. "Yeah, he passed through here about a week back. Folks noticed him soon enough—wasn't exactly tryin' to stay hidden."

Nash nodded, absorbing the information, feeling a flicker of satisfaction at the confirmation. "Did he say where he was headin'?"

he bartender shook his head. "Didn't say much of anything, just kept to himself mostly. Been another couple of men in askin' after him as well, guess they are trailin' him as well."

Nash frowned, folding the poster back into his pocket. "Other men?"

The bartender nodded. "A few bounty hunters came through a couple days after him, askin' around, just like you. They were lookin' to bring him in, dead or alive, if you take my meanin'." He leaned in a bit closer, lowering his voice. "Cain's got a price on his head in more than one place, and that means there's a fair crowd sniffin' after him. He's got himself holed up somewhere not far from here, tryin' to shake folks off his trail."

Nash felt a surge of grim satisfaction. "Any idea where?"

The bartender shrugged, pouring himself a shot of whiskey and downing it in one smooth motion. "Just rumors."

Nash slid a dollar across the bar; the bartender took it, examined it for a second, and then said. "Some say he's hidin' out in the old mine shafts up in the hills, others claim he's been spotted further west, near a place called Black Rock Canyon. Wherever he is, he's layin' low. Guess he knows what's comin' for him."

Nash glanced around the saloon, noting a few patrons watching him with cautious curiosity. The whispers, the sidelong glances—all of it made clear just how much Cain's presence had unsettled the town. He could feel the tension in the air, the uneasy awareness that a dangerous man had passed through, leaving his shadow behind.

"Appreciate the help," Nash said.

The bartender pocketed it with a nod. "Good luck findin' him. You'll need it. And, word of advice? Keep your guard up. Cain's got a way of slippin' out of tight spots, but he won't hesitate to drag someone down with him if it gives him an edge."

Nash nodded, the bartender's words settling into his mind like stones. He thanked the man and stepped back out into the bright sunlight, the town's silence pressing in around him again as he mounted his horse. The lead was thin, but it was enough. Black Rock Canyon was a good day's ride west, and if Cain was holed up there, he'd be expecting trouble. The mines were closer, and it made sense to go there first. Other bounty hunters were already closing in, their tracks woven into the trail he now followed. This was no longer a solitary hunt—he was part of a chase that had drawn a crowd.

With a last look over the town, Nash set off, his horse's hooves kicking up dust as he headed west. The road ahead was long, but he felt a steely determination settle over him, guiding him forward. He wouldn't stop, not until he'd found Cain and ended this trail of blood and betrayal for good.

The ride to the mines took the better part of the day, the sun high and unforgiving as Nash wound his way through narrow, rocky trails, the dust clinging to his skin and coating his mouth. By the time he reached the old mine shafts, the landscape had taken on a rugged, desolate feel, the hills dotted with scattered heaps of rock and abandoned equipment. The place looked long forgotten, the entrance to the mines yawning open like the mouth of a sleeping beast, dark and still beneath the faded wood supports.

A few prospectors were scattered around, each man deeply focused on his work, scraping through rock and earth with worn hands and tired eyes. Their camps were makeshift—a few bedrolls tossed down, a couple of tents flapping in the breeze, and the odd pot hanging over a smoldering fire. Nash dismounted, tying his horse to a scraggly bush, and approached the closest prospector, a wiry old man with a face weathered by sun and years of dust.

The man looked up as Nash approached, his eyes sharp beneath the brim of a battered hat. "What brings you out here?" he asked, pausing in his work, a rusted pickaxe resting across his knee.

Nash pulled the folded wanted poster from his coat, holding it up so the prospector could see the face staring back in ink. "Lookin' for a man named Cain," Nash said, his voice steady. "You seen him around these parts?"

The old man squinted at the poster, studying Cain's face for a long moment before shaking his head, spitting into the dust. "Can't say I have," he replied, glancing back up at Nash. "What's a fellow like that want with an old place like this?"

Nash shrugged, tucking the poster back into his pocket. "Some folks mentioned he might be layin' low in the hills. Heard he could be around these mines."

Another prospector nearby, a younger man with a heavy beard and a skeptical look, stepped over, glancing between Nash and the old man. "If he's hidin' out here, he's doin' a damn good job of it," he said with a snort. "We've been workin' these shafts for weeks. Place is so quiet you could hear a rattler move if it was anywhere close. Ain't seen a soul but the other men here, and sure as hell nothin' like him."

Nash felt a wave of frustration but kept his expression neutral, scanning the area as if Cain might somehow appear from the shadows. "You sure? He might've passed through without lingerin'," he pressed.

The young man shook his head. "If he had, we'd have known. Ain't much passes by out here without everyone hearin' about it. This place may be deserted, but we all look out for each other when someone new's around."

The older man nodded in agreement, scratching his head. "You lookin' to bring him in, then? Cain's a name that draws trouble, if it's the same Cain I'm thinkin' of."

"That's the plan," Nash said, his tone clipped. "And I don't mind trouble."

The old man chuckled, the sound dry and rough. "Well, best of luck to you, then. I'd say check further west, past these hills. Ain't much here but dirt and old bones, anyway."

Nash nodded, tipping his hat to the prospectors. "Thanks for the help."

With a last look at the dark mine shaft, he turned back to his horse, his thoughts racing. It seemed he'd hit a dead end here, but he was getting closer, the trail narrowing by the day. Cain wouldn't hide forever, and Nash would make sure he didn't slip away this time.

As he mounted up and headed west, he couldn't shake the feeling that Cain was out there somewhere, watching, waiting, and as the sun began its descent, making long shadows across the rugged landscape, Nash pushed forward, determined to stay on the trail, no matter where it led him.

CHAPTER THIRTEEN

The ride to Black Rock Canyon was rough, the terrain growing more jagged and treacherous as Nash pushed his horse forward. By the time he rode into town, the sun had dipped low, casting deep shadows that stretched across the dusty streets. Black Rock Canyon was a small, rough-cut place—little more than a few buildings clinging to the rocky landscape, its saloon the only real sign of life in the fading light. A few men lingered outside, sharing quiet words and sidelong glances as Nash passed by.

He tethered his horse and stepped into the saloon, his eyes adjusting to the dim, smoky interior. The place was alive with murmured conversations, the faint clink of glasses, and the low chords of a piano player in the corner. Nash made his way to the bar, ordering a drink, his gaze sweeping the room. A few heads turned his way, but most patrons were too caught up in their own business to pay him much mind.

As he took a sip of his whiskey, two men entered the saloon, their boots heavy on the wooden floor. Nash felt a quiet prickle of awareness, catching their sharp, assessing glances as they took in the room. They were bounty hunters—he could tell by the way they moved, eyes scanning with the practiced wariness of men who'd spent their lives on the trail. They headed straight for the bar, and Nash watched as they exchanged a few words with the bartender, who nodded toward him.

The taller of the two, a wiry man with sun-creased skin and a scar running down his jaw, sidled up to Nash's left, his eyes sharp as he studied him. The other, broader and quieter, positioned himself on the other side, his gaze cool and appraising. Nash lifted his glass in a silent greeting.

"Lookin' for someone?" the scarred man asked, his voice low and steady.

"Same as you, I reckon," Nash replied, tilting his glass back and taking a slow sip. "Goes by the name of Cain."

The two men exchanged a glance, their expressions guarded but interested. The scarred man signaled for a round of drinks, and soon, all three were nursing fresh glasses of whiskey.

The broader man spoke up, his voice as thick and slow as molasses. "Folks around here don't much like to talk about him," he said, his words measured.

"But they say he's been sighted not far from here. Cain's got a knack for dodgin' trouble, though. Ain't an easy man to pin down."

Nash nodded, his gaze steady. "Figured as much. Heard some rumors up in Godson, thought Black Rock might be worth a look."

The scarred man gave a faint smile, though it didn't reach his eyes. "Seems Cain's a popular man these days. Draws quite the crowd." He paused, tipping his glass in a half-toast. "But can't say I'm too inclined to share any hard-earned leads. This game's got enough players without handin' over the cards."

Nash chuckled, mirroring the man's toast. "Fair enough. Cain's got a price worth chasin', so I reckon we're all on our own here."

They shared drinks and casual talk for the rest of the evening, each man watching the others with quiet suspicion. Nash tried to gauge what the pair knew, but they were careful, deflecting questions with practiced ease. He picked up on hints—fragments of stories about Cain's last known whereabouts, rumors of hidden camps out in the hills—but nothing concrete. The two men were experienced hunters, and they weren't about to give anything away.

147

As the night wore on, the saloon grew quieter, the patrons drifting out one by one. The two bounty hunters eventually took their leave, giving Nash a nod as they headed upstairs to the small rooms rented out above the bar. Nash lingered a little longer, finishing his drink before heading to the small room he'd booked for the night.

In the gray light of early dawn, Nash awoke to the sound of footsteps outside his window. He rolled out of bed, pulling on his boots and glancing out just in time to see the two bounty hunters slipping quietly down the street, saddlebags packed, their horses already tied up and waiting. They moved with the silence of men accustomed to early starts, aiming to put as much distance as they could between themselves and any competition.

A faint smile tugged at Nash's lips as he watched them mount up and ride out of town, unaware of his eyes on them. They'd tried to shake him off, to leave him in the dark—but Nash had no intention of letting them get ahead.

He dressed quickly, grabbing his gear and heading out into the cool morning air. By the time he saddled his horse and hit the trail, the two hunters had a solid lead, their tracks faint in the dawn light, but distinct enough to follow.

Nash kept a steady pace, staying just far enough back to remain unseen. He tracked them through winding paths and narrow passes, the sun rising higher as they ventured deeper into the rugged terrain. The land grew rougher, the brush thicker, and Nash found himself weaving between rocks and trees, his focus sharp as he stayed on their trail.

By midday, they'd reached a secluded ridge overlooking a narrow valley. Nash pulled up just short of the ridge, dismounting and tethering his horse out of sight. He moved forward on foot, crouching low as he crept up to the edge, peering over to see the two men scanning the valley below.

The broader man pointed toward a cluster of trees along the valley floor, gesturing animatedly as he spoke in hushed tones. Nash couldn't hear their words, but he could tell from their posture, the urgency in their movements, that they'd found something—a trail, a camp, maybe even Cain himself.

Nash felt his pulse quicken, his fingers brushing the grip of his Colt. He waited, hidden in the shadow of the ridge, watching as the two men descended the slope, moving quickly and carefully toward the cluster of trees.

He knew he had a choice: he could charge in now, join them in the search, or he could hang back, waiting to see if their lead was solid. He'd been on Cain's trail long enough to know the man was clever, slippery as a fox, and Nash wasn't about to walk into a trap without knowing the lay of the land.

He settled back, his eyes fixed on the valley below, watching as the two hunters moved forward, their figures growing smaller with each step. The hunt for Cain had just taken a new turn, and Nash knew he'd have to be sharper, quicker, if he wanted to come out on top. The trail was hot, and for the first time, he felt like he was closing in on Cain, the final reckoning drawing ever closer.

CHAPTER FOURTEEN

Nash crouched low behind the rocks at the ridge, his gaze fixed on the distant trees below where the two bounty hunters had disappeared. The minutes stretched long, the valley's quiet pressing in around him. A faint wind stirred, rustling the brush and carrying the sharp scent of dry earth, but aside from that, there was only silence.

Then, the first gunshot cracked through the air.

Nash's hand instinctively went to the grip of his Colt, his body tensing as he pressed himself closer to the rock. Another shot rang out, and then another, until the sounds of gunfire echoed through the valley in a jagged rhythm, sharp and urgent, filling the silence with deadly purpose.

He tried to make out what was happening below, straining to see past the trees and rocks, but the dense foliage made it nearly impossible to catch a glimpse of the fight. All he could do was listen, counting each shot, each pause, as if the rhythm might reveal some clue as to who was winning and who was losing.

151

For a few moments, the shots came fast and fierce—then suddenly stopped, leaving only an eerie quiet that seemed to settle over the valley like a shroud. Nash held his breath, listening intently, his gaze never wavering from the spot below. No voices drifted up, no movement stirred the brush—just silence.

He waited, his mind turning over the possibilities. If the bounty hunters had managed to take Cain down, he'd see them returning any moment now, dragging their prize back up the trail. But if they didn't return...

The thought settled heavily in his mind. If Cain had killed them, he'd be slipping out now, taking his chance to disappear back into the maze of rocks and trees. Nash knew Cain's methods well enough by now to guess that he'd leave behind the bodies seeping blood into the dust and empty shell casings left for the wind to cover.

The minutes ticked by, each one pulling Nash closer to the conclusion he'd been dreading: the bounty hunters were dead, and Cain was somewhere down there, likely on the move again.

Keeping his steps light and silent, Nash rose from his cover, moving slowly along the ridge, his Colt drawn and ready. His horse tethered behind him out of sight. He kept low, hugging the rocks and using every bit of cover as he made his way down the slope, his senses on high alert for any sound or movement. Every step brought him closer to the scene of the fight, closer to the danger that lay hidden in the quiet valley.

As he neared the trees, he caught a faint glint of metal among the rocks—a rifle lying abandoned in the dirt, its stock splintered and streaked with blood. He moved closer, careful not to disturb the ground around it, his gaze scanning for any sign of Cain or the hunters. But there was no one.

Then, as he crept forward, he spotted the first body—a bounty hunter, the younger one he'd met in the saloon, his broad form lying twisted in the dust. His hand was still clutching his revolver, his face frozen in a grimace, a bullet hole clean through his chest. Nash crouched beside him, taking a moment to search for any sign of life, but the man was gone, his trail ending here among the rocks.

Further ahead, partially hidden by a thicket of brush, lay the second hunter, the older, scarred man. His hat had fallen off, and his face was turned toward the sky, his eyes vacant and staring. Blood darkened his shirt, pooling beneath him in a stark, final statement. Nash studied the scene, piecing together the fight from the scattered shell casings and the positions of the bodies. It had been quick—Cain hadn't given them much time to react.

Nash rose slowly, his gaze sweeping the area as he took in the aftermath. There was no sign of Cain, but the tension in the air told him the man couldn't be far. He knew Cain well enough to know he wouldn't waste time lingering; he'd be putting as much distance as he could between himself and this scene of carnage.

Nash's eyes narrowed, his grip tightening on his Colt as he stepped forward, picking up the faint trail Cain had left. A scuff of boot prints in the dust, a broken branch leading deeper into the canyon, away from the narrow valley. Cain's escape had been hasty, and it had left a trail.

Nash's gaze lingered on the bounty hunters for a moment, a brief nod of acknowledgment to men who had sought the same justice he was after. They'd come close, close enough to push Cain into a desperate move, but they hadn't been fast enough in the end.

With a quiet breath, Nash straightened, his focus sharpening. Cain was close, and for the first time, Nash felt the thrill of the chase within reach. He would follow the trail through the canyon, silent and steady, one step at a time, until he caught up.

Nash moved carefully back up the ridge, his steps sure but quiet as he went to where he'd left his horse tethered among the rocks. The air was still heavy with the tense silence that had fallen after the gunfight, and as he approached his mount, he cast a glance back toward the place where the two bounty hunters lay. Their lives had ended quickly, violently, at the hands of the man he was now tracking, and the urgency of it settled over him like a dark cloak.

He untied his horse, giving the animal a gentle pat on the neck, then led it down to where the rifle lay abandoned in the dust near the scene. The weapon was a solid piece, its stock scratched and splintered where one of Cain's bullets had hit it, but it was still serviceable. He lifted it, feeling its weight in his hands, a cold satisfaction settling over him. It was more firepower than he'd come into the canyon with, and he knew that against a man like Cain, he'd need every advantage he could get. It wasn't his Henry, but it was about to help him get that back from Cain.

The bounty hunter's saddlebags were scattered nearby, and Nash quickly rummaged through them, finding a box of cartridges. He took what he needed, slipping the shells into his own pockets, then loaded the rifle, feeling the cold click of the chamber as he locked it into place.

These were tools he could use, and Nash wasn't about to let them go to waste.

With the rifle slung across his shoulder and his Colt secured at his hip, Nash mounted his horse, urging it forward as he scanned the ground, looking for the faint traces of Cain's hurried escape. The scuff of hoof prints led deeper into the canyon, down a narrow trail edged with jagged rocks and tufts of dry brush. Cain had moved fast, but not carefully—he'd left broken branches and crushed grass in his wake, enough for Nash to follow.

As he rode down the canyon trail, the air grew cooler, the high walls of rock casting long shadows over the ground. The scent of sagebrush and dry earth filled his lungs, and he kept his eyes sharp, scanning every rock, every shadow for movement. Cain was out there, somewhere ahead, he knew Cain would believe he had killed his pursuers and would be moving fast, not bothering about how much of a trail he left, sure that by the time anyone followed it he would be long gone. That was his style, Nash had followed Cain on enough occasions away from scrapes that he'd got them into to know what he'd do.

The path twisted and narrowed, forcing Nash to slow his horse, but he never took his eyes from the trail. He spotted fresh hoof prints in a patch of softer earth, then a faint smear of blood on a low-hanging branch—a sign that Cain, too, might have taken a hit in the fight. The knowledge fueled him, each clue drawing him closer, guiding him through the maze of rock and shadow. If Cain was hit that would slow him down.

Time blurred as he tracked Cain through the canyon, his focus sharp, every sense honed to the quiet sounds of the landscape. He noted each change, each shift in the trail; it was easy to follow—a disturbed rock here, a partial hoof print there. Cain was smart and cunning, but in his haste, he'd left just enough behind for a man as determined as Nash to follow.

The sun began to dip toward the horizon, casting the canyon in deep, ruddy hues. Nash finally spotted something ahead: a patch of disturbed ground near a narrow alcove in the canyon wall. He dismounted, his rifle at the ready, and moved forward on foot, his steps cautious as he approached the area.

A quick scan of the ground confirmed what he'd suspected. Cain had stopped here briefly, perhaps to catch his breath or to tend to his wound, and the faint impression of his boots led off toward a narrow, hidden path that wound deeper into the rock. Nash's pulse quickened, his resolve hardening. Cain was close, closer than he'd been in days.

The canyon was growing dim in the fading light, shadows stretching long and dark across the rocks as Nash scanned the ground before him. A quick survey of the area confirmed what he'd suspected: Cain had stopped here, likely to tend to a wound. Faint impressions of boots marked the dusty ground, leading toward a narrow path that twisted deeper into the rock, almost hidden from view. Nash's gaze fell on a small smear of blood and a bloody fingerprint on a low stone. The sight sent a thrill through him, sharp and satisfying—Cain had been hit. He was hurting, perhaps slowing down.

Nash followed the trail cautiously, his Colt ready, as the path narrowed and led him gradually out of the canyon. The ground shifted from rock to earth, the terrain opening onto the wide plains just as the last light of day slipped beneath the horizon. The open expanse stretched before him, a vast, shadowy sea under a sky darkening to indigo. He paused, staring out over the silent, endless plains, the air cooling quickly as night settled in.

He knew it wasn't wise to push forward now. Following Cain's trail in the dark was asking for trouble; every rock and dip in the ground would be a hazard, and Cain would have the advantage of setting an ambush if he was lying in wait. Reluctantly, Nash made a quick camp, laying out his bedroll in a small patch of scrub, where he could still see the trail Cain had left. He didn't build a fire; the smell of smoke could drift towards Cain. The minutes ticked by in tense silence as he stared into the dark, alert for any sound.

Then, just as he was settling in, a single gunshot shattered the quiet night.

Nash's head jerked up, his hand instinctively going to his Colt as he strained his ears. The shot had come from somewhere far out in the plains, the sound echoing faintly in the night air. He couldn't see anything, but he was sure it had to be Cain. Cain wouldn't have fired unless he'd needed to; either he'd run into something—or someone—or it was a warning shot to throw off any pursuers.

The night passed slowly after that, and Nash lay awake, his thoughts racing, wondering what Cain was up to. But he stayed put, resisting the urge to venture out into the darkness. Morning would bring better chances and fewer risks.

When dawn broke, Nash was already up, his gear packed and ready. He set off, picking up Cain's trail where he'd left it, the marks on the ground clear in the early light. He moved at a steady pace, each step filled with purpose, his mind sharp and alert.

After an hour, the terrain began to shift, and he caught sight of something ahead—a rough homestead, sitting alone on the plains like a forgotten outpost. Wisps of smoke curled up from a chimney, thin tendrils rising against the blue sky. A figure moved near the entrance, and Nash's pulse quickened. It was a small, ramshackle building, but he could see the dark shape of a horse tethered in the shade beside it.

Cain's horse.

Nash's grip tightened on his Colt as he slowed his pace, scanning the homestead carefully, studying every inch of the place. He stayed low, keeping to the sparse cover of rocks and brush as he approached, his eyes never leaving the figure moving by the doorway.

It was Cain.

Nash's heart pounded, his senses alive with the thrill of the chase drawing to its end. This was it: he'd trailed Cain across miles of rough country through dust and gunfire, and now, as the sun rose over the plains, he knew he was finally closing in.

CHAPTER FIFTEEN

Nash dismounted slowly, his gaze fixed on the rough homestead in the distance, smoke rising from its chimney, Cain's horse tethered in the shade beside it. He led his horse behind a cluster of rocks and a few sparse trees, tying it securely out of sight. With a final pat on the animal's neck, he turned and began his approach on foot, his body low, every movement silent and controlled.

He used the scant cover of rocks and tall grass, his eyes never straying from the homestead. His heart was steady, his pulse a low thrum in his ears. Cain was close—wounded, maybe lying in wait. The thrill of the chase hummed through him, mixed with a sharp edge of caution. He'd tracked Cain this far, but now he was entering dangerous territory.

As he crossed a shallow dip in the land, keeping his profile low, something caught his eye—a dark shape sprawled face-down in the dust, just a short distance from the homestead. Nash stilled, studying the figure, his grip tightening on his Colt. The body lay motionless, arms splayed, legs twisted

161

awkwardly, the edges of a coat lifting slightly in the morning breeze.

The single gunshot he'd heard in the night echoed in his mind, and he felt a cold certainty settle over him. This was the victim of that shot—whoever it was had met their end on this lonely stretch of land, brought down by Cain.

Nash crouched behind a low rise, keeping his eyes on the body as he edged closer. From his position, he could see the telltale signs of a brutal end: a dark stain that had spread beneath the figure, the unnatural stillness of death. The victim was likely a farmer judging by the plain clothes, now dusty and streaked with blood.

A flicker of anger sparked in Nash's chest, a reminder of the kind of man he was hunting. Cain didn't just kill for survival or self-defense; he left a trail of bodies like this, ordinary people caught in his path, sacrificed for his convenience. This was a man who used violence as his currency, and he'd killed without a second thought just to secure his hiding place for the night.

Nash forced himself to stay focused, his mind clear and intent. He moved forward again, staying low, his eyes darting between the body and the homestead. The door was slightly ajar, creaking faintly in the breeze. There was no movement inside, or shadow cast in the doorway, but Nash could feel it: Cain was inside, waiting or resting, biding his time. He'd seen him the night before, and his horse was still tethered at the side of the building in the shade.

He inched closer, finding cover behind a half-broken fence post, his eyes narrowed as he studied the angles. If he approached from the side, he'd have a better chance of getting close enough without alerting Cain.

The silence stretched long and taut around him, broken only by the slight noise of rustling leaves and the creak of the door swinging slowly back and forth. Nash tightened his grip on his Colt, his breath even as he prepared for the final approach.

Cain was close—so close—and this time, Nash was ready.

As Nash crouched behind the broken fence post, his fingers grazing the rough wood, a soft and familiar, quiet voice seemed to drift through his thoughts. It was his mother's voice, gentle but firm, speaking to him in the language of her people, her words a memory woven deep into his mind.

"Be patient, Nash. The land will reveal what you need. The wind and the silence are allies if you listen to them."

He stilled, letting the words settle over him like a calming hand on his shoulder. The sun was climbing, casting sharp angles across the land, but he kept his position, his gaze fixed on the homestead. He knew that Cain was inside, hidden from view, and the temptation to rush in, to end it, was strong. But his mother's words reminded him of something he'd nearly forgotten—Cain was a predator, and predators were dangerous when cornered.

He had water with him, and the cool canteen pressed against his hip reassured him. He could wait as long as he needed; he was in no rush. Cain, injured and likely exhausted, would eventually need to show himself and step out into the open, exposed.

Nash took a slow, steadying breath, his eyes scanning the shadows around the homestead, watching for any flicker of movement, any sign of Cain stepping into view. He could almost hear his mother's voice again, reminding him of the times they'd tracked deer through the forest, moving silently for hours, only to wait until their target finally revealed itself. Patience was as much a weapon as his Colt, and he would use it well.

The wind shifted slightly, a gentle breeze carrying the faint scent of smoke from the homestead's chimney. Nash remained still, feeling the dust settle around him, the sun warming his back as he crouched. Every sound, every shadow became part of his watchful stillness, and he felt a rare calm take hold, a certainty that he could outwait Cain. The land itself was his ally, offering cover, silence, and endurance.

The minutes turned into hours, the morning sun climbing higher, casting shorter, harsher shadows. Nash felt the strain in his legs, the tautness in his back, but he didn't move. His breath was steady, his heartbeat even, his focus unbroken. He knew that Cain wouldn't stay hidden forever, that his patience would wear thin, his need for water or food would eventually force him into the open.

In the stillness, Nash's thoughts drifted back to his mother's words, her lessons on watching and waiting, on reading the land like a story written in dust and wind. The hunt was more than just speed or force; it was about listening, about letting the land guide you.

The door of the homestead creaked slightly, and Nash's gaze sharpened, his body tensing as he watched the slight movement. But no one stepped out, and the door swung back, the silence settling once again. He resisted the urge to shift, to act. He knew now, with quiet certainty, that he could wait as long as it took. He would be a shadow in the landscape, unseen and patient, his presence blending with the rocks and brush around him.

Cain was close, close enough to taste victory, but Nash wouldn't let himself rush. He'd learned too well the price of impatience, and this time, he would heed his mother's voice, the lessons of his heritage. He would wait, and when Cain finally revealed himself, Nash would be ready.

The sun had begun its slow descent, casting long, golden shadows across the landscape, softening the harsh edges of the rocks and brush around Nash. The day's heat had faded into a warm, steady glow, and Nash felt a calm settle over him as he lay in wait, his gaze never straying from the homestead. His patience had held, his mother's words guiding him through the long hours, his eyes steady on the weathered door.

Finally, just as the sun was low enough to paint the world in hues of amber and rust, the door to the homestead creaked open. Nash's focus sharpened, his breath stilling as he watched the faint movement, the shadows shifting in the doorway.

Cain stepped out, his silhouette framed against the dim light inside. He moved slowly, cautiously, his gaze sweeping the area, searching for any sign of danger. Nash stayed perfectly still, blending into the shadows cast by the rocks, his Colt held steady at his side, his eyes narrowing as he took in the figure of the man he'd been hunting for so long.

Cain's posture was different than usual, his shoulders hunched slightly, favoring his left side. Nash could see the faint stiffness in his movements, the careful way he held himself as he stepped out onto the rough ground. A dark patch stained the side of his shirt, and though Cain's wound didn't seem severe, Nash could tell it was enough to slow him down, to keep him from moving with the fluid ease he usually commanded. It was a small advantage, but it might be all Nash needed in a situation like this.

Cain took a few steps away from the door, pausing to scan the land, his hand resting on the butt of his revolver, his gaze hard and wary. Nash could feel the tension in the man's stance, the way he seemed ready to draw at the faintest sign of movement. Cain was no fool—he'd likely known someone would track him down eventually. He was prepared and watchful, but the strain of his injury was clear, a faint hesitation in his steps, a grimace he couldn't quite hide.

Nash remained hidden, his breath measured and silent, every instinct telling him to stay low, to wait. The shadows lengthened, casting the world in shades of deepening gold and shadow, and he watched as Cain took another step forward, his gaze still sweeping the land, his jaw tight with the suspicion that he wasn't alone.

Cain was vulnerable and alone, and Nash felt the weight of the moment settle over him. He'd come all this way, crossed miles of rough country, tracked Cain to the edge of the world, and now, as the light faded and the night crept in, he had his chance.

CHAPTER SIXTEEN

Nash moved carefully, circling the homestead with silent, measured steps, his muscles coiled and ready. Every inch of him was alert, his gaze fixed on Cain as he closed in, his Colt drawn, the metal cool and steady in his grip. He knew Cain's ruthlessness well enough to understand that one slip, one miscalculated move, could instantly turn the tables. Cain was a survivor, a man who had wriggled free of more deadly situations than Nash could count. He wasn't about to underestimate that instinct.

As he moved, Nash's eyes caught on something propped against the wall just out of Cain's reach: a worn rifle and, beside it, his own Henry. His heart quickened. Cain had stripped him of that rifle what felt like a lifetime ago, and seeing it there, so close, felt like a piece of himself returned. He could tell by the distance that it was just out of Cain's immediate grasp, another advantage, small but vital.

He continued his approach, silent as a shadow, until he was close enough to make his move. Cain had turned his back to him, scanning the plains, his hand resting cautiously on the butt of his revolver. Nash leveled his gun, the deadly stillness of the air heightening the tension as he aimed directly at Cain's back. He felt the power of the moment, the culmination of weeks of pursuit, of betrayal, of tracking and trailing this man across unforgiving terrain.

His voice was steady and cold, cutting through the silence like a knife. "Hands up, Cain."

Cain froze, his shoulders tensing as the words settled over him. For a split second, there was a sharp, electric pause, then slowly, he raised his hands, his fingers spread in a gesture of surrender. He didn't turn around, but Nash knew there would be a smirk tugging at the corner of his mouth, a twisted hint of amusement beneath the wariness in his stance.

"Well, look who caught up," Cain drawled, his voice low and mocking. "Took you long enough."

"Step away from the wall," Nash commanded, his voice as steady as the gun in his hand. "Slow and easy."

Cain complied, his hands still raised as he took a few careful steps forward, his body held rigid with tension. Nash kept the Colt trained on him, his gaze flicking briefly to the rifles resting against the wall, ensuring that they remained out of Cain's reach. The man's shirt was stained dark with blood along his side, and Nash could see the faint tremor in his shoulders, the wound taking its toll.

"You made quite a mess along the way, Cain," Nash continued, his voice flat. "Left bodies in your wake without a second thought. Thought you could run forever, didn't you?"

Cain let out a low chuckle, barely turning his head, his voice a mixture of defiance and bitterness. "I told you once, Nash—survival doesn't come cheap. You do what you have to, or you end up dead in a ditch."

Nash's jaw tightened. "And now it's come to this. All those lives, all that running...for what? A moment like this?"

Cain's smirk faded slightly, but his voice held steady. "Maybe. But you don't know a damn thing about me, Nash. You think you've got me cornered, think this is justice, but you're just like every other fool that's chased me. And it always ends the same."

Nash felt a surge of anger at Cain's words, the cold arrogance, the sneering disregard for every life he'd taken. But he forced himself to remain steady, his hand unwavering, his voice calm.

"You're wrong, Cain. This ends here."

Cain turned his head slightly, his gaze meeting Nash's eyes dark and calculating. For a split second, Nash could see the flicker of something—fear, maybe, or just raw defiance. But before Cain could speak again, Nash took a step forward, his voice hard and final.

"Down on your knees," he ordered.

Cain hesitated, his jaw clenched, but Nash's Colt left him little choice. Slowly, with a reluctant scowl, he sank to his knees, his hands still raised. Nash kept his distance, every muscle tense, his instincts sharp as he watched Cain's every movement, knowing that a man like him would take any opening, any chance to turn the situation.

"Tell me," Nash said, his voice a low, cold rasp. "Was it worth it? All that running, all that killing?"

Cain's mouth twisted into a bitter smile. "Maybe not. But better men than you have tried to bring me down, Nash. And they all failed. So if you're thinking about taking me in, just remember—you'll be looking over your shoulder every step of the way."

Nash met Cain's gaze, a steady calm settling over him. He knew Cain was a master manipulator, skilled in turning people's doubts and digging into their fears, but it wouldn't work this time. Nash's resolve had been forged in the fires of betrayal, and he was done playing Cain's games.

"I'm not them, Cain," he said quietly, leveling the gun, his voice a calm promise. "And I don't scare easy."

Cain's gaze flickered, a hint of uncertainty breaking through his sneer. Nash saw something else in the man's eyes for the first time, something close to defeat.

He kept his Colt steady, the quiet finality of the moment filling the air.

As Cain lowered himself to his knees, hands still raised in feigned surrender, Nash felt a fleeting sense of victory, his focus locked on the man he'd pursued for so long. But in the split second it took to blink, Cain's hand twitched, and a glint of metal flashed from his sleeve. Before Nash could react, a sharp crack shattered the air—the unmistakable pop of a Derringer.

Instinct took over as the bullet whizzed past him, grazing his side with a stinging burn. Nash jerked back, gritting his teeth as he felt the scrape of the round cut through the edge of his shirt. He staggered, just a half step, but it was all Cain needed. In that split second of distraction, Cain's hand shot to his revolver, drawing it in a flash as he rolled sideways, diving for cover behind a low wall by the homestead.

Nash cursed under his breath, his mind racing. Cain was no longer in his sight, shielded by the rough stone wall, his body hidden behind its shelter. The calm control Nash had held moments before had been shattered by that one desperate shot, and he knew he couldn't afford to underestimate Cain now. The man was cornered, wounded, but as dangerous as ever—maybe more so, driven by sheer desperation.

Nash pressed himself against the nearest bit of cover, a cluster of rocks, his heart pounding as he adjusted his grip on his Colt. The sting of the graze on his side was sharp, but he forced himself to ignore it, his mind honing in on Cain's position. Dust hung in the air, kicked up from Cain's dive, and the silence between them crackled with tension.

Cain's voice rang out from behind the wall, mocking and defiant. "That all you got, Nash? Thought you were smarter than this!"

Nash ignored the taunt, keeping his breathing steady, his focus razor-sharp. He knew that Cain would try to bait him, to draw him out. He wasn't going to fall for it.

He edged around the rocks, keeping low, his eyes trained on the wall where

Cain had taken cover. The dying light cast long shadows over the landscape, the low sun glinting off Cain's revolver barrel as it peeked out briefly, ready to fire at any movement. Nash took a breath, steadying himself. Cain had shown his hand, revealed his last trick with the hidden Derringer—and now, Nash would have to make sure he didn't get another chance.

The showdown had turned, the chase had quickened, and in this final standoff, there would be no room for hesitation.

The air around the homestead was thick with tension as Nash moved cautiously, his Colt drawn, every nerve alive as he scanned for any sign of Cain. The low stone wall provided Cain with just enough cover to keep out of Nash's line of sight, and each time Nash shifted positions, looking for an angle, he'd catch only the barest flash of Cain's coat or the glint of his revolver.

Cain's voice called out from behind the wall, smooth and mocking, echoing through the stillness. "You really think you're any different from the rest, Nash? I've had tougher men than you come gunnin' for me—and look where they ended up."

Nash gritted his teeth, refusing to let the taunt dig under his skin. He'd heard it all before. Cain's voice was a snake's hiss, calculated to keep his focus fractured, his attention split between the man's words and the next possible angle of attack.

Nash darted behind a wooden rain barrel, the wood was old and brittle under his weight. He steadied himself, peering around the corner to catch a quick glimpse of Cain, but the man was already on the move, ducking to the other side of the wall. Another flash of movement—just a quick shift of Cain's coat—and a bullet splintered the edge of the barrel where Nash had been leaning moments before. Nash returned fire, the bullet pinging off the top of the wall.

"Close, but not close enough!" Cain's voice was a harsh rasp filled with grim amusement. "I figured you for a better shot than that, Nash! Thought your Apache blood gave you some kind of edge."

The mention of his heritage, the cold way Cain twisted it, sent a fresh wave of anger through Nash, but he forced it down, keeping his breath even. This was all part of Cain's game, a last, desperate ploy to unnerve him, to make him reckless. Nash wasn't about to let it work.

Moving quickly, he ducked behind a pile of stacked firewood, keeping his head low. He could feel Cain's eyes scanning, searching for him, and he waited, watching, listening. There was a faint rustle, and Cain shifted again, his shadow cast against the ground as he moved closer to the edge of the wall, just barely within Nash's line of sight.

Nash leveled his Colt, waiting for that one clear shot. But Cain ducked back just in time, and another bullet ricocheted off the firewood, sending splinters flying.

"Not so easy, is it, Nash?" Cain taunted, his tone carrying that dark, infuriating confidence. "You've spent all this time chasing me down, thinking you're some kind of hero. But you're just another fool lookin' for revenge—and revenge is just another way to dig your own grave."

The words rolled over Nash, their poison trying to find its mark. But he remained silent, his resolve cold and steady. Cain might have the advantage of cover, but Nash had something more—patience, clarity, the strength of someone who'd come too far to let words shake him now.

He crept along the side of the firewood pile, moving around the homestead's edge, keeping himself low as he scanned every corner, every shadow. He knew Cain was watching and waiting, and he could almost sense the man's smug smile and the way he thrived on dragging people into his twisted game.

"Come on, Nash!" Cain's voice rang out again, louder this time. "You want this over, don't you? Come out and face me, or keep hiding like the coward you are!"

Nash's jaw tightened, his breath measured as he edged closer to the low wall. Cain was playing to his own strength—bending reality with words, turning the fight into a taunting game of cat and mouse. Nash wasn't going to bite. This wasn't about pride or proving something to a man like Cain.

In the shadows, Nash caught a glimpse of movement—a flicker of Cain's revolver as he shifted, his attention momentarily distracted. Nash seized the moment, firing a shot that struck the wall inches from Cain's head, sending a burst of dust and stone into the air.

Cain cursed, ducking low, his voice sharp with irritation. "So, you got some grit after all," he sneered. "But we both know how this ends, don't we, Nash? You'll wind up like the rest—dust in the wind, another notch on my gun."

But Nash could hear something else in Cain's voice now—a faint edge of desperation, buried beneath the bravado. Cain knew he was running out of options, his cover dwindling with each exchange. And Nash wasn't about to give him an inch of ground.

He moved again, this time circling wide, closing the gap as he kept his gun trained on the low wall. Cain would have to show himself sooner or later, and when he did, Nash would be ready.

Cain's hollow and bitter laughter echoed one last time before fading into silence. In that quiet moment, Nash held his breath, his finger poised on the trigger, ready for the final moment of reckoning that was about to unfold.

Nash moved steadily, his footsteps silent, his body low as he closed in, forcing Cain into a corner with each careful, calculated step. Shots echoed through the fading light as he fired, each one chipping away at Cain's cover, pushing him back and making him scramble for safety. The low wall and scattered rocks offered little refuge, and Nash knew it was only a matter of time before Cain had nowhere left to hide.

Cain was breathing hard, his confidence fraying, the smirk he'd worn before slipping with each gunshot that rang out. His taunts grew quieter, more desperate, until there was nothing left but the harsh breath of a man who knew he'd been bested. Nash's grip on his Colt steady, his mind cold and focused as he edged closer, each shot driving Cain further back, boxing him in.

Cain heard the sound of Nash's boots too late.

He whipped around, his eyes wide, his revolver raised—but Nash was already there, closing the distance with the speed and precision of a man who'd spent every minute of this chase preparing for this moment. In one swift, brutal motion, Nash tackled him, the two of them crashing to the ground in a blur of fists and fury. The impact rattled through Nash's body, but he didn't relent, his focus singular as he grappled with the man who'd betrayed him, stolen from him, and left him for dead.

Cain struggled, his hands scrabbling desperately for his gun, his breath ragged and sharp. But Nash was faster, his hands seizing Cain's wrist, twisting it in a hard, unforgiving grip. Cain's fingers slipped from the weapon, his eyes widening as Nash forced him down, pinning him against the hard earth, his own revolver pressed firmly against Cain's chest.

"Enough games," Nash growled, his voice a low, dangerous rasp that cut through the silence. "You're done, Cain."

For a moment, a flicker of emotion crossed Cain's face—a strange, chaotic blend of defiance and something deeper, a glint of fear mingled with a twisted kind of admiration. He looked up at Nash, his mouth curling into a bitter smile, his chest heaving beneath the pressure of Nash's revolver.

"Well, go on, then," Cain taunted, his voice rough, every word laced with mocking bravado. "Finish what you started. Or are you as soft as I always thought?"

Nash's eyes narrowed, his grip tightening as he pressed the barrel harder against Cain's chest. His heart thundered, his mind racing, but he held steady, refusing to let Cain's words sway him. This wasn't just about revenge or anger—it was about finally ending the cycle of blood and betrayal Cain had left in his wake.

He leaned in closer, his voice a harsh whisper. "You're gonna answer for everything you've done. One way or another, it ends here."

Cain's smile faded as the gravity of Nash's words settled over him.

CHAPTER SEVENTEEN

The road back to town was quiet, a stillness broken only by the creak of leather and the steady, shuffling steps of Cain's horse. The sun was beginning to set, casting long shadows across the dusty trail and painting the horizon in hues of crimson and amber. Nash rode beside Cain, keeping a firm hand on the reins of the outlaw's horse, his mind tracing the path that had led him here.

It had been a choice he hadn't expected to make, certainly not in the way he had imagined. He could've ended it back at that godforsaken homestead, could've left Cain sprawled in the dust as another mark of vengeance on a land already bloodied. But something had shifted inside him. The thought of killing Cain had left him with a coldness he couldn't ignore, a darkness he'd felt creep up too many times over the years. Instead, he'd bound Cain to his saddle, leaving the man to face whatever justice awaited him in town.

The sun dipped lower, casting a golden haze across the landscape. Nash found himself drawn into memories of the past weeks—fighting alongside Cain, the tension building between them, the lies and suspicions that had unraveled their bond. He had learned the hard way to trust his instincts, to listen to the quiet pull of reason over rage, to know when it was time to walk away.

Behind him, Cain shifted, the rope around his wrists chafing against the saddle horn. He was silent, his face drawn in a bitter scowl. The outlaw's expression was set, but Nash could see something else—a sliver of defeat, the hollow stare of a man who'd lost, not just the fight, but everything else he had left.

Cain finally broke the silence, his voice rough. "So this is how you see it? Leaving me to rot?"

Nash didn't look back. "I reckon you made that bed yourself, Cain. I just chose not to bury you in it."

Cain scoffed, though his voice held a note of bitterness. "You got any idea what they'll do to me?"

Nash exhaled, glancing briefly at the man beside him. "Maybe."

For a long stretch, neither man spoke. The wind stirred, carrying the scent of sagebrush and dust, mingling with the fading heat of the day. The town lay in the distance, a smudge of civilization against the open plains, and as they drew closer, Nash felt a strange weight lift from him, a burden he hadn't known he was carrying.

By the time they reached the outskirts of town, the streets were empty, bathed in the pale, fading light of dusk. Nash slowed, guiding Cain's horse to a stop outside the sheriff's office. The building was quiet, its windows dark, and he wondered if the sheriff would even be there. But he felt resolved; he knew this was where their journey together would end.

He dismounted, then turned to Cain, who stared at him with a look that was equal parts anger and desperation. Nash untied the rope binding him to the saddle but kept Cain's hands bound, leading him toward the steps.

Cain paused, his jaw clenched, a flash of something raw in his eyes. "I thought we were partners, Nash," he muttered, the bitterness seeping into his words. "Guess I was wrong."

Nash met his gaze, calm but unyielding. "A partner wouldn't have shot me and left me for dead."

With that, Nash knocked on the sheriff's door, waiting until the man appeared, his expression surprised. The sheriff's gaze shifted between the two men, taking in Cain's bound wrists and Nash's calm demeanor.

"Cain here's got a bounty on his head," Nash said simply, his voice steady. "Figured he's earned his spot behind bars."

The sheriff nodded, and without another word, took Cain by the arm, leading him inside.

An hour later after he'd given the sheriff the information he'd wanted, Nash was sat on a wooden bench outside the saloon, debating on whether to go inside or not. His fingers tapping against the pouch filled with the reward he'd just received for Cain's bounty. The weight of the coins should've been comforting—he'd done what he set out to do, after all. Cain was gone, and with him, the danger he posed. But as he clenched his fist around the pouch, all he felt was a hollow ache that he couldn't shake.

"Is this what you wanted?" the voice in his head whispered.

He squeezed the pouch harder, the metal edges digging into his skin through the leather. He thought of Cain's words, the last ones spoken in the dark when he'd held a the Colt to his chest: "They'll pay you, but it'll cost you more." At the time, he'd dismissed it as desperation, a final ploy to unsettle him. Now, he wasn't so sure.

The sudden creak behind him of the saloon doors jolted him back to the present, and Nash opened his fist, letting the pouch dangle from his fingers. It felt heavy—too heavy. Not just with coins, but with the weight of something he hadn't bargained for.

He knew what he'd tell himself later: that he was just doing what had to be done, that this was the way of things. He knew Cain like he knew himself—too well, perhaps. And with that knowledge came the question that haunted him now: what separated them?

The coins clinked as he set the pouch down beside him, unable to stand the weight of it any longer. He could walk away, leave it behind. But he wouldn't— he knew that. He'd take the money, and he'd live with what it meant, no matter how much it gnawed at him.

But as he picked it back up and made his way through the batwing doors of the saloon he wondered if Cain had been right after all.

The next day the dusty street was alive with a quiet, grim anticipation as Nash made his way toward the edge of town, where a crowd had gathered in a tight, unwavering circle. At its center, Cain stood on the back of an old wagon bed, a noose coiled around his neck, his hands bound before him. The pastor's low voice drifted over the crowd, reciting verses in a steady rhythm, the words of God delivered with solemn finality.

Nash hesitated, just for a moment, his hand stilling on the reins as he watched the scene unfold. He'd brought Cain in himself, handed him over to the sheriff with barely a word, but part of him had thought it would take longer than this. Yet, in a town this hardened by dust and despair, there was no patience for justice delayed. They'd seen enough of Cain's kind, felt enough of his kind of trouble, and they were ready to be rid of him.

Cain's gaze shifted, finding Nash, his face shadowed by the gallows beam above him. For a moment, they locked eyes, and in that single, charged look, a hundred words hung between them—betrayal, anger, regret, and something else Nash couldn't quite name. Cain's mouth curled into a bitter smile, defiant to the end, and he mouthed something, his lips moving in silence. Nash didn't need to hear the words to know their meaning.

"You'll be just like me."

Nash felt a chill roll through him, a whisper of doubt creeping in around the edges of his resolve. But he held Cain's gaze steady, refusing to flinch. This was Cain's reckoning, and he'd earned every inch of it.

Slowly, Nash turned away, nudging his horse forward, his shoulders squared and his jaw set. He heard the crack of the whip behind him, the rumble of the wagon as it lurched forward, and then the quick, sharp snap of the rope as it pulled tight.

The noise faded as he rode away, leaving only the soft rhythm of his horse's hooves on the hard-packed earth and the low murmur of the wind as it swept across the plains. Nash didn't look back, not once, but the weight of the past clung to him like dust.

EPILOGUE

The afternoon sun cast a yellow glow over Hodgson as Nash rode slowly down the dusty main street, his shadow stretching long and thin beside him. The town looked just as worn as it had the last time he'd seen it—leaning buildings, faded signs, and the faint smell of dust and tobacco lingering in the air. But today, it felt different. Today, he wasn't here with Cain at his side or a gun drawn in his hand. Today, he was here alone, carrying only a satchel filled with what he owed.

As he dismounted and approached the general store, memories of that fateful day rushed back—Cain's easy grin, the glint of his revolver, and the tremble in the storekeeper's hands as he'd emptied the cash drawer. Nash's jaw tightened as he stepped onto the creaking wooden porch, and he drew in a deep breath before pushing the door open.

Inside, the store looked just as he remembered, shelves cluttered with goods, the air tinged with the smell of old tobacco and leather. Behind the counter, the storekeeper glanced up, his expression wary as he took in Nash's familiar face. A flicker of recognition crossed his eyes, and his posture grew tense, his mouth settling into a hard line.

"Afternoon," Nash greeted, his voice friendly.

The storekeeper nodded, his gaze steady but guarded. "Afternoon." There was a pause, heavy with unspoken words. "Didn't expect to see you back here."

Nash nodded, swallowing hard. "I reckon I owe you a few things."

He reached into the satchel and pulled out a small leather pouch, placing it on the counter with a firm but gentle motion. "That's the money... and a little extra." The pouch contained not only the cash they'd taken that day but a fair bit more.

The storekeeper's eyes shifted from Nash's face to the pouch, his lips pressed into a thin line. His hands trembled slightly as he picked it up, loosening the drawstring and peering inside. He looked back at Nash, a mix of surprise and wariness in his gaze.

"I... don't know what to say," the storekeeper murmured, his voice barely more than a whisper.

Nash's throat tightened. "That's not all." He reached back into the satchel and pulled out more: two bottles of whiskey, a box of cartridges, several packs of jerky, and a few tins of tobacco, setting each item on the counter in a neat row. Each piece felt heavier than the last as he placed it down, a tangible reminder of the choices he'd made.

The storekeeper stared at the items, his expression softening from suspicion to something closer to understanding. "You didn't have to come back and do this," he said, his voice steady but thoughtful. "Men don't usually come back, especially when they got what they want."

Nash shifted uncomfortably, unable to meet the man's gaze for a moment. "Maybe I didn't," he replied, his voice rough with the weight of his own uncertainty. "But I reckon it wasn't right, what happened. Cain... well, he's gone now. And you didn't deserve what he did that day."

The storekeeper studied him, as if searching for something beyond the words, something unspoken. "And you? Why'd you do it?"

Nash took a deep breath, feeling the tangled mess of emotions roiling within him. "I don't rightly know," he admitted, his gaze falling to the worn wooden floor. "Maybe it's to keep my face off a wanted poster. Maybe it's just guilt. Or maybe..." He hesitated, struggling to find the right words. "Maybe it's just because it needed to be done."

The storekeeper nodded slowly, a small, understanding smile tugging at the corners of his mouth. "Sometimes, it's hard to tell the right reasons from the wrong ones. But what matters is that you came back, and you tried to make it right."

Nash nodded, a weight lifting from his shoulders, though a dull ache remained. "That's what I was hopin'." He gave a slight, weary smile, tipping his hat. "Sorry, for what it's worth."

The storekeeper held his gaze for a long moment, then extended a hand across the counter. Nash hesitated before gripping it, the handshake firm, the quiet understanding between them more powerful than words.

As he turned to leave, Nash felt a strange mix of relief and lingering regret, the weight of his choices still settling within him. He might never fully understand why he'd done it, or if it made any difference in the end. But as he stepped out into the fading afternoon light, he felt a sliver of peace in the knowledge that, for better or worse, he'd tried to set things right.

And as he rode away from Hodgson, he hoped it was enough.

The End

Please don't close the book just yet!

I'd like to thank you for reading, your time has been much appreciated, and I am heartened that you reached the end. This has been a work of love to bring back to life the tales left so many years ago by my grandfather's father in his journals. Stories of the old west, of times long forgotten and from people telling them as recent events. It has been a humbling experience to record these events and bring them back to life nearly 150 years later.

If you could spare a few moments to leave this ol' writer a review, and in doing so you'll be leaving one for the writer of the original journals, **Declan Kelly**, and those whose lives you've read about.

I've been heartened by messages from people who wanted to know more about Nash/Red Cartwright. I'd never thought I'd write more than one of these books, never thought people would read and enjoy them and want to know more. When I wrote the first book it was towards the end of the trail for Nash, but this one is from the first story Nash recounted to Declan.

The next episode from his life is "The Rise of the Gunfighter."

OTHER WYATT STEELE BOOKS

The Trail of the Gunfighter
The Law of the Gunfighter
The Silent Gunfighter
The Revenge of the Gunfighter
The Wrath of the Gunfighter

Printed in Great Britain
by Amazon

55785579R00109